MW01628406

Daisy

Ted Wojtasik

Front cover art: Image Gallery KDP

Acknowledgments

I would like to thank Betsy Dendy for reading this in first draft form.

ISBN-13: 978-1-7360229-3-1

St. Andrews Press

St. Andrews University
(A Branch of Webber International University)
1700 Dogwood Mile
Laurinburg, NC 28352
press@sa.edu
(910) 277-5310

Ted Wojtasik, Editor
Ronald H. Bayes, Founding Editor
1969

Also by Ted Wojtasik

No Strange Fire

Collage

Raking Leaves: Stories Set in Connecticut

My Christmas Memory

Dedicated to

William M. Parker

Table of Contents

Her face was sad and lovely with bright things in it, bright eyes and a bright passionate voice—but there was an excitement in her voice that men who had cared for her found difficult to forget: a singing compulsion, a whispered "Listen," a promise that she had done gay, exciting things just a while since and that there were gay, exciting things hovering in the next hour.

—F. Scott Fitzgerald, *The Great Gatsby*

Obsessions are the most durable form of intellectual capital.

—Eve Kososfky Sedgwick, *Between Men*

Chapter I

A fool. A beautiful little fool. Perhaps Daisy was right. That's the best thing a girl can be in this world—a beautiful little fool. The best thing a good girl can be.

Well, for some girls, maybe, but not all girls, and certainly not for me. Not for Miss Jordan Baker. I am a good girl. After all, it *is* 1922. The Nineteenth Amendment has finally been passed. We can vote, we can work, we can smoke and drink and dress as we want, we can bob our hair and do as we want. There's no need for women to be beautiful little fools, no matter what Mrs. Daisy Fay Buchanan thinks just because she prefers to be one. The only time being a beautiful fool works is if you happen to be a beautiful little *rich* fool. And that's what Daisy is. That's how she managed—and manages—to live her life. That's her handicap as she moves from green to green, obstacle to obstacle, hazard to hazard.

I had planned to play golf that afternoon—in fact I was *dressed* to play golf—

when Nick called up, suddenly, after weeks and weeks, to ask if he could stop by to talk. He said he was leaving town. He was returning to the Mid-West. And there we were: Nick sitting in a straight-backed chair leaning forward slightly as he talked or occasionally getting up to move restlessly about the room, while I sat comfortably and perfectly still in a big soft easy chair to listen to him.

All those questions from the summer stirred up once again. Daisy and Tom. Gatsby and Daisy. Tom and Gatsby. Metaphorically Nick had to place that same record on the Victrola and drop the needle on the vinyl to play it over and over again, listening intently to the music and the movements and the occasional discordant note to see if he could hear some new rhythm, some new beat, some new sound that would help him to appreciate or to comprehend what the composer had intended. For me that summer had been jazz, Nick, jazz, Nick—spontaneous, improvisational, crazy, and thrillingly gay.

At one point early in the conversation, he said, "Years ago, my father gave me some advice. It's one of those things that just sticks in your mind. He said, 'Whenever you feel like criticizing anyone, just remember that all the people in this world haven't had the advantages that you've had.'"

Nick looked at me to see how I would evaluate that nugget of Benjamin Franklin counsel.

When I didn't respond, he continued, "And I have had advantages ... as *you* have, Jordan. More than most people."

"But, Nick, can't some advantages be a *dis*advantage?"

That stopped him for a moment. "I suppose ... yes, I suppose that's true."

"You know, Nick, Aunt Sig once gave me some advice, too. She told me, 'It's good to have a set of morals,'" and I paused for effect, "'because then you know what to laugh at.'"

I looked at him to see how he would register *that* information. His face stiffened and his lips, those usually kissable lips, pressed together slightly whenever he was considering some thought or proposition.

"So," I continued, "the question is what are we laughing at here? What's here to laugh at? Or what was *there* to laugh at?"

My Aunt Sig. Mrs. Sigourney Howard. It's lucky I came to the East Coast when I was seventeen to live with her because the best golf courses and the best players were in the East, and my professional career was just about to take flight. Aunt Sig welcomed me as though I were her own child—she was married and divorced twice but had no children. She managed to fill my head with things distinctly *not* Louisville, Kentucky. She was a suffragist.

She had worked virtually her entire life to get the Nineteenth Amendment passed. She served as a secretary for the National American Woman Suffrage Association for five years, planned marches and rallies, wrote articles for the *Woman's Journal,* lectured and lobbied and campaigned for women's rights. And she did not hesitate to criticize a man ... or a woman, for that matter. "We're not on this good earth to be characters in *Little Women,*" she said on more than one occasion.

Nick had stepped over to the window, his hands on the sill, and gazed down at the traffic below. "Is there anything *not* funny?"

I did not move. He felt I was being flip, cynical, jaded. His back had that brooding hunch to it. He was searching for some moral or some meaning from this summer. Searching through the exhilaration and madness and turmoil of these past three months, he had to turn over each incident, each fact, each revelation seeking for the answer to some unanswerable question.

"Is that a rhetorical question, Nick? Let's not have a bum time."

He turned from the window with an enigmatic expression stitched on his face. "If you only knew all the details. Everything. Then it might make more sense."

I thought I did know all the details ... or as many as I needed to know. He sat back down and leaned forward again to talk. To talk about Daisy, about Tom, about Gatsby, about us. I only half-listened to him. I suppose the only great question in life is how we cause each other much sorrow. For Nick, the love affair—that strange thing—between Daisy and Gatsby represented some ingenious metaphysics that would somehow justify the sad wreckage of this past summer. And what *did* happen? An affair that went bad. A set of circumstances that erupted into violence. A foolish woman and a foolish man pursuing a foolish dream.

But how is it possible that Gatsby made Daisy Fay Buchanan the object of all his desire? How is it possible that his vision would consume all facts and realities and all oppositions without alteration? How is it possible that a man could not believe that the past is past and best left alone? That the future cannot *be* the past? What type of romantic idealism is that? Perhaps that formed part of the tragic attraction. Who knows?

Nick clearly wanted to know. That's the reason he's here. That's the reason he's sitting in that chair opposite me. He wanted to pick over each detail of the summer to set it into some pattern or some whole to comprehend its meaning. He was always so serious, so sincere.

His secret pride, he once told me, was his honesty.

I had laughed then, I really couldn't help it, and said, "If you're honest, you just are. You don't have to *say* that you are." His face had become a document of perplexity. "That just makes a good girl suspicious, Nick. Besides, you don't want to have honesty—you want to have a kind of *terrible* honesty."

I think that might have been the moment—I can't remember the exact moment but this one was as good as any—when I first thought Nick reminded me of a Boy Scout. The Boy Scouts of America. God, that organization must be ten years old by now. Another male fraternity of oppression that began, of course, in Great Britain, stressing mental, moral, and physical development with its blatant militaristic trappings. Nick has that same capacity for moral imperialism—a type of naïve and earnest belief in his own rightness. Perhaps I could become a Boy Scout. Wouldn't Aunt Sig just love that? Or I could start up my own fellowship called the Beautiful Little Fools of America.

I interrupted. "Have you heard from Daisy?"

Nick sat back and looked at me. "No, I haven't heard from them since ... since Gatsby was killed. I called them the day Gatsby died, but they left earlier that afternoon."

I said slowly, "I knew they were leaving."

"You did?"

"When I left that morning, Daisy told me that she and Tom were going to go away for a little while."

"Did she say where?"

I shook my head.

"Did she say when they would return?"

I shook my head again. "I haven't heard from them either."

What did it matter where they went or when they returned? To the South Seas, to Paris, to Toronto. This week, this October, next June. Just that they left. When there's any type of trouble, they pack up and they leave. And then they return when they return—*if* they return.

"I saw Gatsby that morning," Nick said. "Before I left for work. To see if he needed anything. He was waiting to hear from Daisy. She never called up. I suppose he never heard from her."

"I don't think so, Nick. I think the only calls they made that morning were for taxis, trains, and travel agents."

Nick slowly shook his head and folded his hands in his lap, looking down at them.

Tilting my head to the side to peer at him more intently, I asked, "Do you think Daisy *should* have called Gatsby?"

"I don't think it would have mattered, actually, at that point."

"True ... some things just settle themselves without interference."

He kept his eyes focused on his hands folded in his lap. Nick did have nice hands, long slender fingers and clean bright nails. I tilted my head back up straight and let my eyes wander over the ceiling. Whether Daisy had called up or not called up? Would it have made a difference, or would it *not* have made a difference?

Daisy Daisy Daisy. Daisy still remained at the center of this whole utterly remarkable smashup. The object of Gatsby's vision. The center of Gatsby's life. The meaning for Gatsby's existence. Without Daisy there was no Jay Gatsby—and Jay Gatsby, as it turned out, was himself a self-creation.

But who was Daisy Fay of Louisville, Kentucky? Aunt Sig always snorted or harrumphed or shook her head, in a goodhearted and sympathetic manner, whenever I mentioned the Fay household. Daisy was hardly the type of woman Aunt Sig admired or could ever remotely respect, and Aunt Sig was hardly someone Daisy admired or respected, always calling her a senile old thing a thousand years old, which is far from the truth: her mind is a sharp as a thorn. Daisy was not a suffragist or a feminist or an independent-minded woman. She was hardly even a flapper. Oh, yes, she adopted a few superficial traits—the dress, the smoking, the bobbed hair—to appear modern, but she was content to center her life on ... possessions. To be dependent upon men and money. To have a beautiful mansion and numerous servants and lavish jewels.

How I used to admire her back in Louisville! But certainly no more. All in all, Daisy is a rather frivolous, materialistic, shallow woman. Didn't anyone see her for that? Didn't Gatsby? Didn't Nick? Really? She simply remained that silly eighteen-year-old girl racing around in her white roadster and kissing all those soldiers. A Gardenia girl. She just never changed. That was her problem. And she had no other goal than to be pampered and spoiled and coddled.

At least I had my golf bag, a set of good clubs, and one hell of a swing. Thank God I had Aunt Sig. I left Louisville for Manhattan in a pleated plaid skirt and white blouse with bright visions of moon and magnolias. Within weeks, it seemed, I changed. I became a professional athlete. I became competitive. I groomed myself to be independent, self-sufficient, ironic, and often sarcastic. I voiced defiance of expectations. I approached life with a fearful honesty. Unlike Daisy, my goal was *not* to submit to the institution of marital bliss. For me, marriage was simply subordinate, incidental, a fond afterthought. God forbid—to think I might have turned out to be just another Daisy Fay Buchanan. But Daisy, for some reason, had to have been more than just that. I suppose she had to have been for Gatsby to pursue her with such persistence.

Nick shifted in his chair, having made some point, that I only half-heard.

"That green light," he was saying. "To have bought that monstrous mansion to be right across the bay from her."

"What green light?"

"At the end of their dock. Didn't I ever tell you about that night after I met you?"

And he told me. The arms, the trembling, the reaching. I wondered then if Nick himself had been consumed by Gatsby's dream as well. And he told me about the walk through the house, about the shirts and her tears—I knew about the shirts already. "I couldn't help think at the time that there had to have been moments when Daisy fell short of his dream—not through any fault of her own but because of the extraordinary vitality of his hope."

"Life is not a series of holes-in-one," I said in a matter-of-fact and rather flat tone of voice.

"What's that?"

I repeated my statement. "That would be lovely, but it's not reality. We always hope for a hole-in-one but realize that they are rare, rare occasions. Every golfer has that intense type of expectation: this one might be a hole-in-one. And when it's not, we just continue the game."

Nick smiled. "And Gatsby?"

"He was hoping for a hole-in-one. That didn't happen."

His smile faded. "And us?"

"We never knew each other's handicap."

He sat silent.

"Besides, Nick, I'm engaged now." That wasn't strictly true, but it certainly felt like an engagement. And I told him to whom.

He just looked at me with no expression, stood up, and moved to the window again to stare down at the traffic.

"Nevertheless you did throw me over," I said and stood up. "You threw me over on the telephone. I don't give a damn about you now, but it was a new experience for me and I felt a little dizzy for a while."

I stepped toward him, and he turned around.

"Oh, and do you remember," I added, "a conversation we had once about driving a car?"

"Not exactly."

"You said a bad driver was only safe until she met another bad driver? Well, I met another bad driver, didn't I? I mean it was careless of me to make such a wrong guess. I thought you were an honest, straightforward person. I thought it was your secret pride."

I knew he simply thought me an arrogant bitch for that remark, but wasn't his insistence upon that Boy Scout honesty also arrogant?

"I'm thirty," he told me. "I'm five years too old to lie to myself and call it honor."

I didn't respond. His face seemed to wrinkle in sudden anger and anguish, but he merely murmured goodbye, shook hands, and turned away.

"I can let myself out," he said, and he was gone. Gone back to the Mid-West. Gone as he had left me that night poor Myrtle Wilson had been killed.

I stood alone in the parlor. I doubted I would ever see Nick again. I was surprised, really, to have seen him even now. It was time, simply, to let it go. Aunt Sig told me once, "To live in this world, you have to do three things: to love what is mortal, to hold it tight against your bones knowing your life depends upon it, and when the time comes to let it go, let it go." That time had come.

I wandered over to the window that Nick kept looking out of and peered down into the street. I thought I saw him climb into a taxi, but I couldn't be sure.

To let it go. Gatsby could not do that.

I straightened, stood erect, poised. For some reason, I looked at my golfing gloves, those fingerless gloves to help my grip. To dream about that hole-in-one.

Would it really help to think more and more about Daisy and Tom and Gatsby? And Nick? To confront this past summer with renewed scrutiny? Was there really anything to gain from that?

The days were so much shorter now, darker so much longer now. I can still hear Daisy asking that silly question about the longest day of the year the first night I met Nick: "Do you always watch for the longest day of the year and then miss it?"

I missed it that summer. We all missed it. I don't know. Maybe I did miss something that summer and that's why Nick was here. We all missed something that summer: Tom, Daisy, Gatsby, Nick ... me. But Nick needed to know what it was. He needed to know.

"Do you always watch for the longest day of the year and then miss it?" I suppose the entire summer really did begin that bright June evening.

Chapter II

Early in June, on a warm windy evening, Mr. Nick Carraway first arrived at Tom and Daisy's mansion for cocktails, who was some second or third cousin of Daisy's from the Mid-West. I was staying with the Buchanans that week. I needed a retreat from Manhattan. That morning, after breakfast, I sank into one corner of that enormous white sofa in the parlor and watched as Daisy murmured into the telephone.

"Nick, darling, is this really you?"

She paused and listened intently, a satisfied smile pulling at her mouth.

"Who *else* could you possibly be? Oh, I don't know." Daisy spoke in that coy whispery voice she often adopted. "A mysterious stranger claiming to be a distant cousin of mine who wants to steal my daughter and sell her into white slavery?"

She tilted her head at his response.

"No? You won't?"

She nodded.

"Then you must come over and steal the silver. You can at least steal the silver, can't you?"

She paused.

"Oh, good. I need some excitement, Nick," she announced—a conspiratorial summons evident in each syllable of each word. "Come over and steal the silver immediately. Tonight. At dinner. Of course, tonight, darling. I couldn't bear to have another minute pass without seeing you."

She laughed and listened. "Not one minute more, Nick. We're here for good now. Here in East Egg. Tom and I ... and Pammy. My beautiful little girl. All together in our new home!"

And so, later that day, Daisy and I lay on that enormous white sofa while Tom strode—he always seemed to be striding that summer—to the front porch to greet our dinner guest for the evening.

Tom still had on his riding outfit. He still does have a sturdy body and a sturdy step, a brutal step, in some ways, but he hasn't really changed physically all that much since they first married. He just seemed somehow ... fuller, as though his physique had over the years simply expanded with muscle and cockiness and dominance. He was still wearing his riding outfit to impress this Nick Carraway, Daisy's distant cousin, but he also I think went to college with Tom.

Anyway, horses, ponies, hunting, racing, steeple chasing—that's the glory of Tom's life now. And he has to make his mark: the black boots, the tight breeches, the swanky shirt. It's such a costume for Tom ... or a type of uniform. It's not merely boots and breeches but a firm declaration of centuries of breeding, sportsmanship, and superior life choices. Always to make an impression—the same way this mansion here was to make an impression.

I could just scarcely hear Tom's confident voice retelling his perfected Demaine-the-oil-man-story routine. "I've got a nice place here," he said. I could see him move that broad hand of his about like some military dictator, indicating the front vista, the sunken Italian garden, the half-acre of roses, and the motorboat bumping against the dock. He'll sweep that hand of his here and about and then announce, abruptly, directly, in a matter-of-fact-but-please-take-exceptional-notice tone of voice—"It belonged to Demaine the oil man"—as though that statement explained everything, affirmed everything. That entire sweeping gesture of his says boldly and brashly that it's mine, it's mine, it's mine, can't you see? So much like a cat spraying its territory. But it *is* a lovely place, I must admit—a gorgeous house, in fact. And I must say that I'm pleased and grateful to have a guest room here, all the time, when I absolutely must get away from the city.

When Tom strode out of the room, he seemed to pull in his wake a sudden strong gust of wind that swirled from one end of the room to the other—a cool muscular summer breeze. The curtains at both French windows shuddered and shook and flapped upward toward the ceiling. With my head tilted back, I lay and watched the fluttering shadows from the curtains foxtrot with the ceiling's scrollwork directly above me. Then the breeze slipped into me, whispering into my white cotton dress (designed by Chanel, of course) as I half-closed my eyes and imagined myself a weightless shadow as well, fluttering and shifting along the ceiling. I had closed my eyes to mere slits when I heard Tom's sturdy step in the hallway and a lighter, more tentative step beside it.

With my head back and my chin tilted upward, as though it were a tee with a golf ball balanced on its top, I waited for Tom and the guest. I know I have a good profile. God knows, I have seen enough pictures of it in the papers and magazines, but I have ceased to think about it. That is one of the first rules of flapper charm: to be perfectly groomed and dressed so that one simply forgets about it. Well, forgetting about my profile and my body and becoming a mere shadow, I just felt languid and indolent lying there under the spinning blades of the ceiling fans.

Through my eyelashes I gazed over at Daisy lying opposite me, also dressed in a white dress. For all intents and purposes, she was still that lovely young vivacious girl I so used to admire in Louisville. She still had those beguiling blue eyes, good high color, and honey blonde hair, cut short now like a flapper, though she hardly fits the image, being married to Tom and subservient to him and all his money. In some ways, she seemed like some medieval princess who had been locked up in some gloomy castle tower and the key tossed into the moat. There's really only one flapper in this room, but Daisy would screech to hear me say so.

I heard Tom, in a louder voice, announced, "We'll go inside."

The steps stopped at the entranceway. Through my slitted eyes I could see Daisy and, peripherally, Tom and the guest. One more gust of wind slapped through the room and sent the curtains swirling upward and as though borne up in that swirling Daisy and I were swirled upward too.

Tom strode over to the French windows at the far end of the room and shut them with a bang—the whip and snap of curtains and the breeze itself died out. That's Tom to a tee: with one decisive gesture, he kills anything that's lovely and alive.

Daisy turned her head and placed a hand down firmly on the edge of her fluttering dress. I merely opened my eyes, just a bit more, but did not move a muscle. Tom stood there in front of the French doors as the captured breeze quivered and died out.

Daisy leaned up and forward and laughed—that absurd little laugh she has that some men find so charming, alluring, delightful, a laugh that should be patented and sold by street vendors all through the city—and Nick Carraway laughed, too, as he stepped into the room toward her.

"I'm p-paralyzed with happiness," Daisy declared and laughed again as she held Nick's hand for a moment, looking up into his face.

"And that lazy creature," Daisy murmured in as low a voice as possible, "is Miss Jordan Baker."

A quizzical look wrinkling his brow and eyes, Nick bent toward her—I'm sure he only hears the words "lazy" and "Baker" clearly. I think the rumor that Daisy murmurs so softly to make people lean close to her is true. Did she think I couldn't hear her? Of course not, it's all in good fun. I don't mind what she says about me.

I moved my head, just a little, and mumbled, "'ello."

Nick looked over at me, with that same quizzical expression on his face, almost as though he were about to apologize for disturbing me or as though I had spoken in a foreign language he did not know. He is a rather handsome man in the manner of a Brooks Brothers advertisement. I wonder if he recognized who I am. He must. Most people do. My pictures are all over the place. The Fairway Flapper. Known for her fierce competitiveness and grim determination. I've become entirely independent and self-sufficient, thanks to Aunt Sig, but I also learned that most men publicly admire those qualities in a woman but privately resent them. Well, it's a new world: the war is over and the Nineteenth Amendment is now law.

I wonder if this Nick Carraway will admire or resent, privately, those qualities. Daisy did discuss him earlier in a positive fashion, but I don't necessarily trust her judgment in men. He does have a rather kissable mouth.

"Nick, darling," Daisy went on, "how *are* you? And how did you ever end up on Long Island? I suppose Tom pointed out every little detail of the place, didn't he?" She glanced at Tom who still stood near the French windows as though he were a guard. "And let me ask you? Did he by any chance mention the name Demaine?"

"As a matter of fact, he did."

"Oh, of course he did," Daisy declared laughingly. "How could he not? Demaine the oil man, Demaine the oil man. That's his summer song, my darling. I hear they sing it up and down Broadway and in all the speakeasies. When he first told me, do you know what *I* said?"

"I couldn't imagine."

Daisy gave him that coy practiced look of hers. "Demaine *who*?"

Nick laughed lightly. Tom had started to move about the room. I still remained as I was watching this small staged entertainment with interest.

"Tom was quite furious, as though I were belittling the name of our Republican representative or plotting the overthrow of the American government. He's become very serious. Haven't you, Tom, haven't you become very serious?"

Tom did not answer when Nick looked over at him. Nick was decidedly not a sad bird: dark hair, almost black, and slicked back with generous amounts of pomade; slender and straight-standing, as though he were an athlete, but his hands were too soft and too manicured for anything beyond a recreation tennis match; intelligent and innocent eyes, set a little too close perhaps, but with a certain glimmer of mischievousness; and a white shirt, lightly starched, and cuff-linked with onyx.

When Tom didn't respond, Nick turned back to Daisy and told her that he had stopped off in Chicago for a day or so on his way east and that a dozen people had sent her their love.

"Do they miss me?" she cried in ecstatic, rippling notes.

"The whole town is desolate," he said and bowed slightly. "All the cars have the left rear wheel painted black as a mourning wreath and there's a persistent wail all night along the North Shore."

"How gorgeous! Let's go back, Tom. Tomorrow!"

Well, I must say that this Nick Carraway does know how to banter. He should get along just fine with this crowd.

Then, a *non-sequiter*, Daisy added, "You ought to see the baby."

"I'd like to," Nick answered politely.

What else could someone say? No, I could care less to see some whiney tiny brat.

"She's asleep. She's two years old. Haven't you ever seen her?"

"Never."

How would that even be possible?

"Well, you ought to see her. She's—"

Tom placed a hand on Nick's shoulder and asked him a business question. "What're you doing, Nick?"

Always business and money and horses, horses and money and business and Demaine the oil man.

"I'm a bond man."

"Who with?"

I couldn't catch his answer, but Tom remarked, "Never heard of them."

"You will," Nick answered, a shortness in his voice. "You will if you stay in the East."

"Oh, I'll stay in the East, don't you worry," Tom said, glancing at Daisy and then back at Nick as if he were alert for something more. "I'd be a God Damn fool to live anywhere else."

Oh, I've just about had enough of Tom's talk.

"Absolutely!" I said with suddenness and a certain forcefulness.

Nick started. Daisy stared at me. Tom turned toward the couch. I yawned, somewhat unashamedly, and in a series of rapid, deft movements stood up.

"I'm stiff," I complained. "I've been lying on that sofa for as long as I can remember.

"Don't look at me," Daisy returned. "I've been trying to get you to New York all afternoon."

To shop and chatter and chatter and shop. No thank you.

The butler, as if on cue, appeared all of a sudden with a tray of cocktails.

When he offered me one, I said, "No thank you. I'm absolutely in training."

"You are!" Tom said with an incredulous look and drank down his drink. "How you ever get anything done is beyond me."

How Tom even manages to talk is somewhat beyond me. But I do manage to get things done. I manage to get quite a few things done. And I have that tournament tomorrow. Someone, I forget who, said once, "Idleness cures all ills." Not that I'm ill, but that idleness is delicious.

I stood for a moment motionless, as though I had just stepped onto a tee box to evaluate the fairway with my shoulders back and my back straight. Some magazine once said that I had a jazz-nourished figure—slender and erect and supple—and I glanced with mild curiosity at this Nick Carraway to see if he appreciated that observation. With that single glance, I could tell that he found me attractive or, at least, gay and interesting. My hair is blond like Daisy's, but a duskier hue, and bobbed, of course, but thank God I don't have blue eyes: I have grey eyes, which are certainly more distinctive. I'm sure he recognized me now, standing there straight, since all I would need is a golf club to complete the tableau.

I turned to him then and said, with just enough of a challenge in my voice, "You live in West Egg. I know someone there."

"I don't know a single—"

"You must know Gatsby."

"Gatsby?" Daisy exclaimed abruptly. "What Gatsby?"

I was about to tell her that Gatsby was this preposterously rich man who had dropped into Long Island like a hole-in-one when, suddenly, the butler appeared again.

"Dinner is served, madam."

Daisy turned to him. "Oh yes, yes, thank you."

Tom grabbed Nick's arm and seemed to push him out of the room. Daisy and I set our hands lightly on our hips, like two good gardenia girls, and sauntered out to the porch where dinner was being served. In the diminished wind, four candles flickered against the sunset.

"Why *candles*?" Daisy said with a frown and with her fingers snapped them out. "In two weeks, it'll be the longest day in the year. Do you always watch for the longest day of the year and then miss it? I always watch for the longest day in the year and then miss it."

That's Daisy. Always missing something. Watching and waiting for something but always missing it. How much has that girl missed in her life?

"We ought to plan something," I said in a rather pragmatic voice but could not help yawning the words as I sat down at the table. I wish I were just getting into bed.

"All right." Daisy took it up. "What'll we plan?" She turned to Nick. She couldn't turn to Tom. "What do people plan?"

Oh, we could climb on pogo sticks and hop down Fifth Avenue or play mah-jongg in Central Park. Before Nick—or anyone for that matter—could respond, she shifted her blue gaze to her little finger. "Look! I hurt it."

We all looked at it. The knuckle was black and blue. Ah, a hazard.

"You did it, Tom," she said. "I know you didn't mean to but you *did* do it. That's what I get for marrying a brute of a man, a great big hulking physical specimen of a—"

"I hate that word hulking," Tom said crossly. "Even in kidding."

I wonder what Tom's handicap is on *this* fairway. I didn't want to have a bum time, so I asked Daisy what she had wanted to do in the city this afternoon. Sometimes Daisy and Tom's quarrelsome life together bores me senseless.

Dismissing Tom's remark with a slight shrug, she turned to me as we started to chat easily about really nothing at all, while Tom and Nick talked equally easily about bonds and the Yale Club and the various business activities in the city. Could this Nick possibly be as dull as Tom? Perhaps he *is* a sad bird. His earlier banter with Daisy indicated otherwise, so this must be the veneer of politeness—I hope. They did go to Yale together, that much I found out, so Nick must be 28 or 29.

The plates appeared and disappeared: the watercress soup, the salad, the Boeuf en Daube, those dull pears in chocolate.

"You make me feel uncivilized, Daisy," Nick said, having sipped more of his claret. "Can't you talk about crops or something?"

Here we are. The inarticulate farmer's boy who goes to Yale to become articulate. The Feel of the Soil. *O Pioneers!* and Sherwood Anderson rolled into one. It was a good gambit but Tom, being Tom, missed the entire gambit.

"Civilization's going to pieces," Tom said, even more violently than usual. "I've gotten to be a terrible pessimist about things. Have you read *The Rise of The Coloured Empires* by this man Goddard?"

"Why no," Nick responded, his face stirring with interest and unease. "Should I?"

"Well, it's a fine book and everybody ought to read it. The idea is if we don't look out the white race will be—will be utterly submerged. It's all scientific stuff. It's been proved."

Daisy reacted with her usual sarcasm. "Tom's getting very profound. He reads deep books with long words in them. What was that word we—"

"Well, these books are all scientific," Tom continued with an impatient glance at her. "This fellow has worked out the whole thing. It's up to us who are the dominant race to watch out or these other races will have control of things."

"We've got to beat them down," Daisy said with a wink.

I may as well join this nonsense. "You ought to live in California—"

However, Tom interrupted, shifting heavily in his chair. "This idea is that we're Nordics. I am and you are and you are and—" After a moment he included Daisy in this chain of association, and I'm glad Daisy winked once again at Nick. "—and we've produced all the things that go to make civilization—oh, science and all that. Do you see?"

Tom and his scientific theories. All that rant about superior races, studies, civilization. He's been on this now for ... oh, I don't know, a month now, but it's all so tiresome. Tom must always be superior. He's such a dullard. Such a sad bird.

I watched Nick's response with keen curiosity. Would he agree with Tom? If he did, I thought I would probably scream, pull my hair out, jump up and down on the table ... then the telephone rang. Tom stopped talking. The butler left. Another hazard.

Her blue eyes blinking rapidly for a moment, Daisy leaned toward Nick and whispered, "I'll tell you a family secret. It's about the butler's nose. Do you want to hear about the butler's nose?"

"That why I came over here tonight."

Nick surprised me. He's playing the game so well. Tom sat tense.

"Well, he wasn't always a butler," Daisy continued. "He used to be the silver polisher for some people in New York who had a silver service for 200 people. He had to polish it from morning till night until finally it began to affect his nose."

I offered, "Things went from bad to worse," knowing this silly little anecdote.

"Yes, Jordan, things went from bad to worse until finally he had to give up his position."

And that's the point. He had to give up his position. He couldn't take things anymore. Tom merely shifted in his seat. The evening sunlight, dying and fading, fell upon her face. Daisy did have a lovely face, and her skin and eyes seemed to glow in the fading sunlight as if the light momentarily illuminated all the sad things and the bright things engraved in her features. I felt such sorrow for her then and all that she had to endure to remain Mrs. Daisy Buchanan.

The butler returned and, leaning down, said something into Tom's ear. Daisy visibly stiffened and the sunlight seemed to slip off her face. Nick sat uncomfortably with his elbows resting on the table, indifferent to what was playing out. How could he not be more interested in what was going on? Tom frowned, pushed back his chair, and strode inside without a word.

Daisy leaned toward Nick again. "I love to see you at my table, Nick. You remind me of a—of a rose, an absolute rose. Doesn't he?" She turned to me for confirmation. "An absolute rose?"

I barely had a chance to acknowledge her remark and her question—which I thought even more foolish a remark than usual since Nick hardly resembled a rose—before she suddenly threw her napkin down onto the table.

"Excuse me," she said and stood up and rushed inside after Tom.

I glanced at Nick with my eyebrows raised with the full meaning of the situation, but he had a bland expression on his face. Oddly enough, he started to say something.

"Sh!" I warned him, sitting up straight and leaning forward, so I could hear better if I could hear anything at all. The words were indistinguishable in the house, but the murmured tones of voices rose and sank and rose again and then just stopped.

"This Mr. Gatsby you spoke of is my neighbor—"

Why in the world was he trying to make small talk? "Don't talk. I want to hear what happens."

"Is something happening?" he asked with utmost sincerity.

"You mean to say you don't know?" I said, quite surprised. "I thought everybody knew."

"I don't."

"Why—" I wondered if I should be the one to tell him about the unhappy and galling situation with his cousin or third cousin or whatever she was to him? "Tom's got some woman in New York."

"Got some woman?" he repeated with a certain blockage of meaning.

I feared I would have to be more blunt, though how I could be more blunt I didn't know so I simply nodded. "She might have the decency not to telephone him at dinnertime. Don't you think?"

Some incomprehension still lingered in his face, but that shattered precipitously and fell from his face into his lap where he placed his hands and sat up straight just as Daisy and Tom returned.

“It couldn’t be helped!” Daisy fairly cried, her voice taut with rhinestone gayety. She sat down and glanced searchingly at me, defiantly. “I looked outdoors for a minute and it’s very romantic outdoors. There’s a bird on the lawn that I think must be a nightingale come over on the Cunard or White Star Line. He’s singing away—. It’s romantic, isn’t it, Tom?”

Things must be worse than I imagined. A nightingale? For heaven’s sakes, Daisy.

“Very romantic,” Tom answered and then, desperate to change subjects, turned to Nick and said, “If it’s light enough after dinner I want to take you down to the stables.”

Then the telephone rang again, if you can believe it. Can that woman be so utterly ill mannered? There must be some name for this kind of brazenness, but what that is I certainly don’t know. I watched both Daisy and Tom with keen interest to see how this second telephone call would be handled.

Daisy shook her head decisively at Tom, and the subject of stables and horses and all subjects actually dried up and drifted away into the gathering darkness. She got out of that trap with a clean shot.

We just sat there in complete silence as the butler, rather needlessly, lit the candles again. I could tell that Nick was extraordinarily uncomfortable, and I wondered if he had ever been exposed to such modern moral turpitude before. Tom’s little affair had certainly developed well beyond a discrete behind-the-scenes adulterous escapade. To have his mistress call the house! That pushes effrontery to a new edge.

I must talk to dear old Aunt Sig about such effrontery. After all, an affair is an affair. Daisy acts as though Tom were the first woman to ever cheat on his wife. But there *are* certain rules to abide by, for heaven's sake, if a man decides to take a mistress. Tom behaves as if he were a character in a late novel by Henry James.

Somehow idle talk ensued and then we all stood to leave the table. The stables weren't mentioned again, so I strolled back into the library with Tom while Daisy and Nick strolled down the veranda to the front porch. To discuss distant-cousin topics, I assume.

Once inside I sat down at one end of the enormous white sofa, picked up a *Saturday Evening Post* from the side table, and flipped idly through it.

Tom sat down heavily at the opposite end. "I suppose Daisy must think me a true—"

"Don't, Tom," I said resolutely, turning a large glossy page. "Not now."

I really just could not bear to talk about it. I have no need to. I've listened to Daisy complain and cry about if for weeks now. I tell her to leave the bastard. Daisy sniffles and says that she can't. I tell her that divorce is quite fashionable these days and it would make her a positive inspiration to others to dump a dull, adulterous husband. She shakes her head. I've listened to her carp about all the other instances of infidelity in his past; those, however, *did* seem to be rather quick disruptive manifestations of male conquests, while this one seemed such a bold break from the simple decent rules of social behavior.

Tom huffed and mumbled, "Well!"

I found a story called "Trust Emily—A Farce Comedy."

"Let me read you the second installment of a story by May Edginton, Tom," I said. "That should pass the time more profitably than discussing what shouldn't be discussed, don't you think?"

Before he could object, I simply started reading out loud. The words just tripped off my tongue and fell into the room. That telephone call ... and the *second* telephone call—the entire situation is unnerving and indecent. I tried to concentrate on my voice and the words, so I wouldn't have to think too much about Tom's woman.

Then, with an upward glance, I noticed that Daisy and Nick were standing in the doorway, but I lifted my hand for them to be silent so I could finish reading the paragraph.

"To be continued," I said, tossing the magazine back on the side table, "in our very next issue."

I've had enough of Tom for one night and babysitting him so Daisy could have some time alone with Nick. I stood up.

"Ten o'clock," I said, stretching and gazing at the ceiling. "Time for this good girl to go to bed."

"Jordan's going to play in the tournament tomorrow," Daisy explained, "over at Westchester."

Sudden recognition bloomed like a rose in Nick's face. "Oh,—you're *Jor*dan Baker."

Ah yes. Jordan Baker. Now he knows. I suppose it is always somewhat unusual to meet someone you've seen only in pictures and only in golf attire. I could see him flipping through a catalog in his mind of just how many pictures he *had* seen of me ... and then a slight wrinkle in his brow that appeared and disappeared and I wondered if he was thinking about that unpleasant incident early in my career—that certainly added to my notoriety ... and mystique.

"Good night," I said in a soft tone. "Wake me at eight, won't you?"

"If you'll get up."

"I will. Good night, Mr. Carraway. See you anon."

"Of course, you will," declared Daisy. "In fact, I think I'll arrange a marriage. Come over often, Nick, and I'll sort of—oh—fling you together. You know—lock you up accidentally in linen closets and push you out to sea in a boat, and all that sort of thing—"

Yes, all that sort of thing.

"Good night," I said, climbing the stairs. "I haven't heard a word."

On the upstairs landing I did hear Tom announce that I was a "nice girl" and ought not to "run around the country" the way I do. I could hear Daisy coming to my defense, as she would, while I strolled down the hallway to my room and away from their words. I have no patience with Tom's primitive ideas about what a "girl" ought or ought not to do. He would have women back in corsets! He would rather I become Daisy, married and homebound and drenched in jewels, as if that were a good life. Poor girl, having to put up with his nonsense. Tom is the type of man who resents any woman having any independence at all, which is a simple threat to his masculinity and to his superior Nordic race. Oh, enough of Tom! This Mr. Nick Carraway does interest me, and I do hope I'll run into him again. That might be fun.

I undressed and slipped into bed, letting the evening swirl through my mind for a few minutes. I thought about Nick and about that horrible woman calling during dinner and about that brute Tom and about flighty Daisy absorbing all the awful shocks of a bad marriage. Then I fell asleep.

I usually fall asleep rather quickly and rather easily and had already entered a dream in which I was swinging my golf club and hitting holes-in-one all down the fairway when I heard

Daisy's voice calling me. She must be in the crowd lining the putting green but why is she calling me when I'm about to putt until I woke up and found Daisy sitting on the side of my bed. I could see her dark profile outlined in the silvery moonlight.

"Jordan, darling, are you very much asleep?"

I harrumphed something and sat up in bed. I did not want to talk about Tom. His girl in town. Not now. "I never sleep, Daisy. I just pretend. Sleep is for actresses."

"What Gatsby?"

"What, darling?" I still had the image of a final hole-in-one in my mind.

"What Gatsby did you mention to Nick?"

"Oh ... just some man who lives in West Egg and throws these gorgeous parties."

"Do you know him?" she asked, somewhat breathlessly.

"I've met him."

"What does he look like?"

"He's handsome. Tall, dark, and handsome. Very mysterious."

"*Ser*iously, darling."

"Oh, he's about thirty or so and he *is* handsome but he's not all that tall and he's not all that dark. Short light brown hair and a deep tan and I don't really know what color his eyes are. But he had this engaging smile. It's the smile that defines him. He *is* mysterious ... no one knows exactly where he comes from or what he does but he has boatloads of money ... and, Daisy, love, I really am quite sleepy and I have that tournament tomorrow."

"That must be the Gatsby I used to know in Louisville," she uttered, in a strange, hushed voice. "That must be *my* Gatsby."

And then I saw him in her white roadster. And then I realized who he was. The moment she mentioned our hometown, everything flashed back to me. *Of course.* "I'm sure that's who he is, darling."

My eyes were closing again, and then they did close, and next I knew I was awake with the morning sun and thinking about Westchester.

Chapter III

Weeks later, at Gatsby's huge circus-like mansion, I stepped outside and stood at the head of the marble steps looking down into the garden and the crush of people surrounding the cocktail table.

"Hello!"

With all the noise I was surprised I could hear one particular "hello" at all. I peered out at the "hello," which seemed so distinctive, somehow, over the music and the voices, and there moving toward me was Mr. Nick Carraway. He was dressed all in white flannels with a cocktail glass in hand and his dark moleskin hair slicked back on his head. He appeared rather dashing, in a swashbuckling kind of way, his face flushed from drink and embarrassment.

I said in an absentminded manner as he came up to me, "I thought you might be here. I remembered you lived next door to—"

I gave him my hand, lightly, to let him know that I would remain with him as we started to descend the steps. First, however, I had to listen to these two foolish girls dressed in identical yellow dresses who stood at the foot of the steps calling up to me.

"Hello!" they cried in unison. "Sorry you didn't win."

I bet. It was a lousy game anyway.

"You don't know who we are," one of the girls said before I could respond, "but we met you here about a month ago."

"You've dyed your hair since then," I said, but no sooner had I made this remark to indicate that I did indeed know who they were, the two bitches had wandered away, so my comment just floated up to the moon. I shook my head slightly at these disappearing girls in yellow dresses and my disappearing comment of acknowledgment and placed my arm in Nick's when we reached the bottom of the steps.

We sauntered through the garden and the stumbling laughter and the syncopated music booming upward into the summer night. Nick does look handsome, and it's so gay to have my arm in his. A tray of cocktails appeared, and I took one and Nick took one, and we both sat down at a table with the two girls in yellow dresses and three other men, whose names, when introduced, were a mere mumbles of indistinguishable syllables.

I turned to one of the girls in a yellow dress next to me. "Do you come to these parties often?"

"The last one was the one I met you at," she replied in a bright voice and, turning to her companion in yellow, said, “Wasn’t it for you, Lucille?”

Lucille nodded vigorously. “I like to come. I never care what I do, so I always have a good time. When I was here last I tore my gown on a chair, and he asked me my name and address—inside of a week I got a package from Croirier’s with a new evening gown in it.”

“Did you keep it?” I asked.

“Sure I did. I was going to wear it tonight, but it was too big in the bust and had to be altered. It was a gas blue with lavender beads. Two hundred and sixty-five dollars.”

“There’s something funny about a fellow that’d do a thing like that,” said her companion in yellow in a tense, eager voice. “He doesn’t want any trouble with *any*body.”

“Who doesn’t?” Nick chimed in.

“Gatsby. Somebody told me—”

I couldn’t help but be interested in this intrigue and leaned forward toward the two girls.

“Somebody told me they thought he killed a man once.”

A cool, delicious thrill passed through me and, it seemed, over the entire table. Now the three men also leaned forward to listen.

“I don’t think it’s so much *that,*” Lucille countered. “It’s more that he was a German spy during the war.”

One of the men nodded to confirm this statement. “I heard that from a man who knew all about him, grew up with him in Germany."

"Oh no," the first girl in yellow said. "It couldn't be that, because he was in the American army during the war." As our attention shifted back to her, she opened her eyes rather wide. "You look at him sometime when he thinks nobody's looking at him. I'll bet he killed a man."

She narrowed her eyes and shivered. Lucille shivered. Even I shivered at the manner in which she announced this, and I'm sure it sent a little shiver through Nick as well. Then, as on cue, we all looked about the garden for Gatsby. Of course, no one saw him.

"You know," Nick said to me a quiet voice, "I haven't yet met this mysterious Mr. Gatsby. I'd like to. At least to thank him for the invitation."

"We'll find him. He's here somewhere."

The supper was being served, so I invited Nick to join my own party at our table on the other side of the garden, despite the fact that Mark, my unfortunate undergraduate date for the evening, was there and no doubt concerned about my absence. My party was a table of East Eggers, slumming for the night, they all remarked, even though they were having great fun.

"Are you tight?" I asked Mark.

"I never get tight."

"Mark is a Harvard man," I said loudly to Nick so Mark could hear.

"Class of '23," Mark responded with nonchalant pride.

"That explains his stoic fastidiousness."

"That explains nothing, Jordan," Mark said, reaching out his hand toward Nick. "Mark Watson, the Fourth."

"Nick Carraway."

"Jordan has a certain sense of humor."

"Only after midnight," I said.

"After midnight, though, Cinderella has to go home," Mark responded.

"But I'm not wearing glass slippers, darling."

"You're not? Why I thought you were!"

The rest of the table sat there primly inebriated and watched the crowd surge and struggle through the garden with unabashed interest, as though they were at a boxing match or touring the Lower East Side to see how the other half lived.

"Let's get out," I whispered to Nick. "This is much too polite for me."

"Fine."

Jordan stood up. "I'm on a quest. Nick lives next door but has not yet been properly introduced to Mr. Gatsby, who so kindly sent him an invitation for tonight's party. We must find the host to thank him. You can understand such gentlemanly behavior, can't you, Mark?"

Mark nodded his head as a cynical expression illuminated his face. "Of course."

"Thank God," I told Nick the minute we stepped a few yards from the table. "I can't stand such prim and proper inebriation."

We searched for Gatsby in the bar. We stood at the top of the marble steps as we looked through the crowd. We hunted for him on the veranda. We couldn't find him anywhere.

Finally, on a whim, we pulled open this important-looking door and stepped into a library. The room was high Gothic, oak-paneled, and self-consciously British, as if it had been transported complete from some manor house in Leeds; indeed, there even seemed to be a Lord included in the package—a middle-aged man, burly and beery, with black horn-rimmed circular spectacles precariously perched on the tip of his nose, who sat drunkenly perched on the edge of a great table, ogling a wall of books.

When we walked into the room, he circled around and leered at me with bold, brazen interest from head to toe. I looked back at him with alluring scorn.

"What do you think?" he asked.

"About what?" Nick answered.

Waving his hand toward the bookshelves he said, "About that. As a matter of fact, you needn't bother to ascertain. I ascertained. They're real."

"The books?"

He nodded in an owlish manner, and I thought his spectacles were about to drop from his face. "Absolutely real—have pages and everything. I thought they'd be a nice durable cardboard. Matter of fact they're absolutely real. Pages and— Here! Lemme show you."

With surprising dexterity, he hopped off the table, scrambled to the bookcase, and returned with Volume One of the *Stoddard Lectures*.

"See!" he shouted with triumph and handed it to Nick, who stared at it with mild incomprehension. "It's a bona fide piece of printed matter. It fooled me. This fella's a regular Belasco. It's a triumph. What thoroughness! What realism! Knew when to stop too—didn't cut the pages. But what do you want? What do you expect?"

Then he snatched the book from Nick, who had been turning it about to show me, and returned it to the bookshelf.

"Who brought you?" he demanded. "Or did you just come? I was brought. Most people were brought."

I stared at him with bemused contempt but did not deign to answer his question. What impertinence! However, he was a rather queer fellow. Imagine studying a man's library to see if it were real. A regular Belasco he called Gatsby. David Belasco. Naturalism triumphs in West Egg. That's a slick analysis of these parties—they do seem "staged" in some ways.

"I was brought by a woman named Roosevelt," he continued. "Mrs. Claud Roosevelt. Do you know her? I met her somewhere last night. I've been drunk for about a week now, and I thought it might sober me up to sit in a library."

"Has it?" Nick inquired.

"A little bit, I think. I can't tell yet. I've only been here an hour. Did I tell you about the books? They're real. They're—."

"You told us."

We shook hands with him and left.

In the garden now everyone seemed to be dancing: the fox trot, the one-step, the Charleston, the Black Bottom. Couples whirled. The music boomed and rolled through the tables and chairs and stockinged legs. Shouts of laughter. Girls, all alone, danced interpretive numbers with shimmering abandon. Waiters hurried and stumbled from table to table. Banjos banjoed. Glasses clinked. A buxom white woman sang an Italian aria. A thin black man sang jazz. Even the two girls in yellow performed a stage act of *Twins*, a baby act popular that year. Exhilaration, mirth, and unadulterated drunken merriment rippled through the crowd and through the mansion and floated up into the summer sky to float with the moon over Long Island Sound.

Swept up in the riotous hilarity, I had forgotten my task of searching out Gatsby for Nick. We were sitting at a table in a far corner of the garden. I was drinking champagne from a glass as big as a finger bowl, while this wretched girl at my side laughed uncontrollably at virtually anything anyone said, when I noticed that Gatsby was sitting next to Nick. How did that happen? He must have wandered over and sat down as I was studiously attempting to avoid any conversation with this foolish girl. Well, at least Nick now met Gatsby. I could hear them talking about France and the war.

I turned toward Nick at a pause in their conversation. “Having a gay time now?”

“Much better.”

He turned back to Gatsby. Men. Men and their stories of war. The War to End Wars. Nick waved his hand in the general direction of his cottage, and there seemed to be some embarrassed exchange of words. All of a sudden, a butler appeared and informed Gatsby that Chicago was calling. Gatsby stood up and bowed slightly to each of us in turn.

He said to Nick, “If you want anything just ask for it, old sport. Excuse me. I will join you later.” And then he was gone.

Nick immediately turned to me. “I didn’t realize that was Gatsby.”

“No? Didn’t he introduce himself?”

“Well, he did. He did introduce himself, but after I made a gaff at not knowing who he was.”

“Oh, that won’t bother him. He’s not like that.”

“I thought he would have been some red-faced, bloated, old man.”

“He’s hardly that.”

"Who is he? Do you know?"

"He's just a man named Gatsby."

"Where is he from, I mean? What does he do?"

"Now *you*'re started on the subject," I remarked with a slight smile. "Well,—he told me once he was an Oxford man." I could see some dim construction of history begin to form in Nick's face. "However," I added, "I don't believe it," and watched that dim construction tumble down.

"Why not?"

"I don't know," I said. "I just don't think he went there."

Nick's eyes, wide open with curiosity and the effects of champagne, gazed steadily into mine. Gatsby certainly did have that effect on people—men as well as women. Everyone seemed to want to know who this man was, how he did what he did, why he threw these lavish and gorgeous parties.

"Anyway, he throws grand parties," I said, "where everyone has a gay time. And I like large parties. They're so intimate. At small parties there isn't any privacy."

As if to underscore my last remark, a great boom of a bass drum echoed throughout the garden.

"Ladies and gentleman," the orchestra leader announced. "At the request of Mr. Gatsby we are going to play for you Mr. Vladimir Tostoff's latest work which attracted so much attention at Carnegie Hall last May. If you read the papers there was a big sensation." He smiled, as though he just said something witty, and added, "Some sensation!"

I laughed as did everyone.

"The piece is known," he concluded, "as 'Vladimir Tostoff's Jazz History of the World.'"

And so the orchestra began with its booms and its bangs and its quivering string notes. Nick turned to face the orchestra, but I noticed that his gaze had drifted to the top of the marble stairs. There stood Gatsby, alone, looking from one table to another with approval.

Gatsby has a rather kissable mouth. He's handsome, certainly, in a glossy magazine type of way, as though he aspired to be one of those men in a Kuppenheimer ad in the *Saturday Evening Post*: the tanned skin, the close-cropped hair, the fantastic suit. But there's something—oh, I suppose that drunken man in the library said it well when he compared him to David Belasco—there's something even "staged" about his person, as though he were being photographed all the time. Oh, I knew Nick would pursue this Gatsby interest. Everyone does. I turned my attention back to the orchestra to listen to Mr. Tostoff's piece.

After the orchestra finished the final movement, everyone in the garden exploded into individual antics that seemed, for some reason, choreographed like some vaudeville routine: dancing, swooning, singing. Well, it was just past midnight. Even Nick appeared more relaxed now, having met the host, just enjoying the night noise and the foolish frolics.

"I beg your pardon," I heard behind me. I turned to the voice. "Miss Baker?"

I nodded.

"I beg your pardon, but Mr. Gatsby would like to speak to you alone.'

"With me?"

"Yes, madam."

I stood up, my eyebrows raised in astonishment at Nick, and followed this proper butler toward the mansion. I knew Nick was watching me, so I walked with a jaunty gait through the tables. I always step with my shoulders back, my back straight, my chin level—a sportswoman's walk.

The butler moved through the great foyer and past a large room filled with people singing and drinking and dancing. Lucille, I think, was pounding on the keys of a grand piano while some other woman stood next to her warbling a Broadway song in a grand stage-hall voice. I followed the butler to that same important-looking door that Nick and I opened earlier—the library—that the butler now opened.

Gatsby was gazing out a window, looking out at the darkness, really, because I doubt there was anything to see. I glanced about the room, wondering if that drunken man with the spectacles was hiding somewhere behind a chair.

"Mr. Gatsby," the butler said, "Miss Baker."

Gatsby turned to me. "Miss Baker," he said, "please sit down," and indicated a sofa, covered in chocolate and yellow silk stripes.

A piece of furniture I hadn't noticed before. I wondered if he had his servants redesign the room for this strange meeting, creating a different set for a different scenario, whatever this scenario was supposed to be.

"A drink?"

"Champagne, please," I said, sitting down, still questioning why in the world I was here.

"Champagne then," he said to the butler who quickly left the room.

Gatsby dragged a chair from behind the large desk and sat down near me.

"May I call you Jordan?"

"Of course, Mr. Gatsby, if I may call you Jay."

He smiled that warm, embracing, intimate smile. "Of course, Jordan."

I glanced at the bookshelves again and could only think of Belasco. This was the setting of a stage, but for what drama? Had Gatsby wished to seduce me? Was this how he did it? I sat with my back straight, my ankles crossed, and waited. I knew something momentous—or at least rather thrilling—was about to happen ... but what that possibly could be I had no idea.

He said nothing for a few moments, which seemed longer than they were, except to thank me for coming to see him. He only began to talk after the butler reappeared with a bottle of champagne, flutes, and a silver bucket filled with ice.

"1901?" Gatsby asked the butler.

"Yes, Mr. Gatsby."

He nodded approval as the butler elaborately uncorked the bottle with the most expensive pop I've ever heard and poured me a glass of bubbly before exiting the room. Gatsby, I noticed, did not drink.

I sipped my champagne, and I had never tasted anything so deliciously exquisite. "This is divine champagne. What is it?"

He murmured some name I didn't recognize. "Only 78 bottles left in the world. Well, 77 now."

"I'm honored to be drinking it then." I sipped once more.

"Jordan," he began, and he smiled again, that smile that reassures and convinces and illuminates your person, "you've been to my parties before?" He didn't so much ask a question as make a statement.

"A few," I replied. "They're rather grand parties."

"Yes," he agreed, his smile disappearing, his voice tense with disappointment. "They are rather grand."

An awkward moment ensued.

He then asked, "What do people say about me?"

The question rather shocked me, but I answered quickly. "You're a man named Gatsby who throws the most lavish parties Long Island has ever seen this century! Why?"

He gave a short laugh. "But nothing else?"

"You mean the rumors?" I asked, lifting an eyebrow. Was that it? Was I supposed to be some sort of spy for him at his own parties? That seemed unusually odd. He certainly doesn't need a virtual stranger to relay various gossip that circulates about town.

He nodded, attempting to analyze my expression, which I left expressionless.

I sipped my champagne. "Nothing that would interest you, Jay."

He laughed again. "Oh, you're quite right on that. Quite right." His gaze seemed to focus somewhere above my head. "Not from the people who come here anyway."

I marveled at what sort of people he wanted to come here. I wasn't sure if I had been insulted. "But you have senators and actors, Broadway singers and film stars, who all come here."

"Oh, yes, they all come. They all come."

"And even professional golfers."

He laughed long and loud. "Yes, Jordan, even professional golfers." He paused. "Are you particular friends with Nick Carraway?"

The question took me by surprise. What did he mean by "particular friends"? I didn't think he meant to imply anything unseemly—not that it would have bothered me.

"I know him. We didn't come together tonight if that's what you're thinking. I met him a couple of weeks ago at a dinner party. He lives next door to you."

"Yes, I know."

"We just ran into each other tonight. I thought he might be here because he lives next door."

"Of course."

I sipped my champagne. Was he interested in Nick? Did Nick have his own mysterious history? This was becoming rather fascinating that Gatsby was trying to find out information about Nick.

"But you do *know* him?"

"I sat with him for dinner and walked around trying to find you so he could thank you for the invitation to your party tonight. He's a regular Boy Scout about manners. He couldn't sit still until he made the proper introduction and offered the proper thanks to his kind host."

Gatsby mused over this.

"I don't know him well, Jay," I continued. "As I said, I just met him a few weeks ago at the Buchanans. He's a cousin of some sorts to Daisy."

And then Daisy's image in my bedroom returned. "What Gatsby?" she had asked. That entire sleepy conversation had dropped from my mind, what with the tournament and all—she had said that Gatsby must be the man she used to know in Louisville. I could see him now sitting in Daisy's white roadster. This must not be about Nick. Not directly.

"You see, I saw the two of you together."

I nodded.

"And you could ... say, talk to him?"

"Yes, Jay, I can talk. I can even ask questions. Make demands."

He nodded with vigor as though I had just explained the economic secret behind the magnificent rise in stocks. All the moving about and around whatever it was that he wanted to talk about. Why were men like this? Never able to ask a simple question but to move about in hints and diversions and asides? I had to find out what he wanted to know about Nick. "This is Nick's first party. He finds the people too amusing."

"Oh, yes, too amusing," he murmured and then looked about the room, letting his eyes roam from shelf to shelf of the bookshelves.

I could hear that drunken man shouting that they were real, absolutely real, this fella's a regular Belasco.

In a quiet voice he said, "I thought she would just show up."

"Show up?"

"Like the others. Like the others who just show up."

I smiled. "Daisy?"

"Daisy," he said. "Yes, Daisy Fay."

He couldn't possibly still be smitten with her, could he? God knows how many soldiers fell in love with Daisy that summer. The phone used to ring off the hook. He was certainly not unique in that regard, but now he wanted to renew his acquaintance? He had been hoping all this time that Daisy would just flutter into the insanity like some ravishing lunar moth attracted to the lights of his party one night? That explained all his looking about and searching through the crowds: he had hoped to see Daisy in his garden, listening to the music, sipping champagne, laughing gaily.

"You'd like to see her again?"

He nodded solemnly.

"Well, Jay, why don't you just ring her up and invite her to a luncheon in New York?"

The mere mention of this suggestion made him stand up, stiff, and start pacing about the room. "I can't do that. No, that won't do at all."

"Why won't that do?"

He continued to pace. "That wouldn't be right, no, not all."

I wasn't sure what was right or not right about a luncheon in New York. "Daisy and I run into New York all the time."

"It can't happen that way."

"What is it that can't happen that way?"

That question stopped him. He stared at me with such an odd intensity and declared, "Our reunion."

I absorbed this simple phrase. Those two words opened doors in my mind that sent the curtains banging and swinging to and fro as those on the first day I met Nick and made me realize that he was *still* in love with Daisy. Is that really possible? After all these years? What a very strange situation. Their reunion. I didn't know whether I should admire him or laugh at him.

"But why *not* a lovely luncheon in New York?" I repeated.

He shook his head and sat down. "I don't want to do anything out of the way! I want to see her right next door."

Now that statement stopped *me*. Another door swung opened and slammed shut. Now I understood. It's this *place* he wants her to see. My knowing Daisy, my knowing Nick, Nick living right next door. "You want to arrange a luncheon at Nick's cottage, so she can see your big house."

"So she can see my big house," he repeated.

How splendid. The competitive male. The preening peacock. How it all bores me.

Gatsby asked, "You say that Nick is a cousin of Daisy's?"

"Yes. Somehow. Second or third or fourth. I don't know. There's some family connection." Which makes the luncheon date an altogether easier proposition. "Nick's also a friend of Tom's. They went to Yale together."

That last comment startled him. His eyes blinked quickly. It seemed as though he were going to abandon the entire notion of a luncheon at that point. He nodded and then started to shake his head. “Maybe not, maybe not.”

“Maybe not what?”

“Maybe I shouldn’t ask you to speak to Nick for me.”

“I didn’t know that you particularly wanted me to speak to Nick. I thought you wanted me to speak to Daisy.”

“Oh no, no, not Daisy. She’s not to know.”

“Not to know what?”

“Not to know about the arrangement.”

I should stop drinking the champagne. I was truly baffled. He evidently saw the confusion in my eyes.

“It’s to be a surprise,” he said, speaking hurriedly, “a surprise for Daisy. You see, I want to tell you my story and then you could tell my story to Nick ... I don’t know him ... to make such a request. I’m going to spend more time with him, of course.”

The conversation was becoming more and more complicated. I felt as though, again, I had become a character in a Henry James novel.

“What story?”

As if I hadn’t asked a question, he went on, “And then I want you to ask Nick if he could invite Daisy to his cottage for tea some afternoon. And then she would be right next door, but she wouldn't know she was right next door."

I was supposed to intercede somehow—to talk to Nick but not to talk to Daisy. "What story?" I repeated.

He stared a moment at the floor before looking up at me. "I have been trying to forget something very sad that had happened to me long ago. Five years ago."

"Five years ago I was a sixteen-year-old girl in Louisville."

"And Daisy Fay was eighteen years old, and the most beautiful girl I had ever seen in my life."

He stood up to pour me more champagne and then began to pace again, moving restlessly through the library, around a table, around the sofa, around the chairs, as he told me his very strange sad story.

"I bought this house, so I could just across the bay from Daisy," he declared, his voice sprinkled with both defiance and entreaty. He stopped and looked at me for my reaction.

I was nonplussed, simply dazed with champagne and intrigue. What type of romantic foolishness, is this? An adolescent boy gazing up at his girl's window? I simply nodded.

"You see, Jordan, I have always loved Daisy and I still love Daisy and I will always love Daisy. And what is important to me is that she still loves me as well. After I left for the war, Daisy ... well, she just got restless and confused

... and married because I wasn't there ... she was young, you see, quite young ..."

His voice drifted off momentarily. Oh, I saw. The egotistical male. The fickle female. This was obviously the man she was going to follow to New York before her family absolutely refused to allow her to travel. This was obviously the man who wrote her that letter the night of her bridal dinner. But she *did* marry Tom. That's the point. The hard fact.

"So I traveled trying to forget," he continued, "trying to forget."

I saw in his eyes a glimmer, something rose to the surface from the depths of his memory, something wonderful and dreamy. "You see, we were pledged to one another."

Pledged!

"And that pledge remains. I have never loved another woman. And I know Daisy has never ... never loved another man"—his voice faltered—"even though she did marry ... all I have done all these years I have done for Daisy."

For Daisy. For Daisy. He sat down and, as though he were giving a lecture in a college classroom, gesticulating and pointing, he rattled on about following Society Columns in the newspapers and magazines, investing money and engaging in financial risk to buy a particular piece of furniture or painting or crystal or piano, and acquiring tailor-made suits and shoes and shirts. All for Daisy. For Daisy.

As I listened I thought about Daisy with Tom when they were first married, when they returned from their South Seas honeymoon, when I saw them in Santa Barbara. She unquestionably loved Tom then ... at least then. Then things changed.

Things changed. Didn't Gatsby realize this? Time does not stand still. All the money or power in the world cannot do that. We move on, we go forward, we embrace the following morning.

After Gatsby told me this tale of love and loss and an eternal pledge, I was rather giddy with his astonishing narrative as well as the champagne. However, Daisy does need something in her life ... "So, should I speak to Nick?"

He stood up and stepped over to the window to gaze out at the darkness. "Not yet. I'm going out in my hydroplane tomorrow morning with Nick. And I have some business to attend to this week. Don't tell anyone just yet. Not yet. I need to know Nick a little bit more before I ask him such a request."

I said, gently, "It's not that much of a request, Jay."

He seemed to consider this. "I'll let you know. Not a word to anyone. Not yet. All things must be in place before it happens."

I nodded. Their "reunion." Underneath it all, he's just a regular tough. I figured that if he had waited this long, he could wait a little longer.

He walked me to the library door and pulled it open. Outside the door I could see Nick and the group I came with at the end of the hall in the foyer in a jumble of departing guests. As some well-wishers stumbled toward us to say how much they enjoyed the party, especially *The Jazz History of the World*, Gatsby's entire demeanor stiffened into extreme formality. He started mumbling thank-you's and old sport's as I sauntered down the hall toward Nick. Mark was calling impatiently for me to hurry! Where had I been? Looked for me everywhere! What a sad bird.

After I walked to the foyer, I whispered to Nick, "I've just heard the most amazing thing. How long were we in there?"

"Why ... about an hour."

"It was—simply amazing," I repeated. "But I swore I wouldn't tell it and here I am tantalizing you." I yawned. I couldn't help it. Sleepiness suddenly overcame me. "Please come and see me. Phone book ... under the name of Mrs. Sigourney Howard ... my aunt ..."

Everyone started to hurry me and call to me, so I waved Nick a jaunty salute as I joined Mark and his party. Nick had to be wondering what in the world I was talking about and just what it was that had claimed an hour of my time—or an hour of Gatsby's time—from the party. Won't he be surprised when he finally hears about it.

Chapter IV

Nick finally rang me up a week or so later, and we started to go to places together. He never once mentioned Gatsby's party—that is, about my hour alone with him in the library—and neither did I. Apparently, judging by Nick's description of various activities, Gatsby was getting to know him better.

I was thrilled with the attention Nick gave me. I had thrown over Mark shortly after Gatsby's party and had started to feel a little lonely. I could also tell that Nick enjoyed the attention that Miss Jordan Baker, professional golf champion, received when we went to various restaurants or shows or New York events. That's the advantage of having one good thing that you can do well. In my case, I can play golf with as much ease as I can fall asleep.

"Do you want to go to a party?" I asked him one morning over the telephone.

"At Gatsby's?"

"Gatsby is not the only one who throws parties, Nick."

"He's not? I thought he was. I thought he cornered the market on parties."

"This party's in Rhode Island." I laughed. "In Warwick. One of my golfing connections. Interested?"

"If you are."

I borrowed a friend's car. It's amazing how easily I can borrow things from people—even a brand-new 1922 blue Buick Special Sport-Touring car. The day started brilliantly. Nick admired the car and was surprised someone would lend it to me. I removed the convertible top, so the wind and sun could play through the car we drove. I don't drive as well as I play golf, but I can get from point A to point B.

As we were driving out of West Egg, we had to stop for a few moments to let some trucks cross the road in that desolate stretch with all the ashes and garbage and railroad tracks, smoking chimneys.

"I hate this place," I said, tapping my fingers lightly on the steering wheel. "It's a virtual wasteland. Why can't they build a road around it?"

Nick didn't say anything. Someone honked a horn behind us. I looked over at the hideous billboard with the eyes.

"And I hate that billboard," I said. "There is no Doctor T.J. Eckleburg anymore, so why doesn't someone just tear it down?"

"The eyes are rather haunting, aren't they? Watching you all the time."

"They're not watching *me*."

"His retinas—they must be a yard high."

I laughed. "I'm glad you don't prescribe spectacles, Nick. Those aren't retinas."

"They aren't? What are they then?"

"Those are the irises. Retinas are at the back of the eyes."

"Oh."

The trucks finally moved out of the way, and we were off again with a jerk and a shake. I could tell Nick did not approve of my driving. I could see the tight look of anxiety on his face every time I drove around a curve or sped up when the road was straight.

Then, somewhere in Connecticut, I drove around a sharp bend in the road and came upon a construction crew working on the shoulder. It happened so swiftly with only so much room to maneuver that my right fender actually flicked a button on one man's coat.

"You're a rotten driver!" Nick shouted. "Either you ought to be more careful or you oughtn't to drive at all."

I thought this rather unfair. "I am careful."

"No, you're not."

"Well, other people are," I said, lightly.

"What's that got to do with it?"

"They'll keep out of my way," I insisted. "It takes two to make an accident."

"Suppose you met somebody just as careless as yourself."

"I hope I never will," I answered, glancing over at him. "I hate careless people. That's why I like you."

I turned my sun-strained eyes back to the road, and I knew our relationship had shifted ever so slightly in that moment. I saw the stunned awareness that emerged in his eyes—those Boy Scout eyes. We didn't talk too much the rest of the way.

When we got to the house, I jumped out and Nick jumped out.

"Aren't you going to put the top back on?" he asked, looking up at the gray cloudy sky. "It might rain."

"Oh, Nick, it's not going to rain," I declared.

Needless to say it did rain, one of those quick hard summer storms. Nick ran out to try to put the top up, but it was too late. The rain ended almost as quickly as it began, and the interior of the car was drenched.

Nick, who was also drenched, looked at me with those smug knowing eyes.

"Don't, Nick."

"Don't what?"

"Don't tell me you told me it might rain."

"I won't then."

I looked at the car. "I'll take care of everything."

The rest of the party went well.

When I returned the car to Horace Stoddard, I told him that someone had borrowed the car in Rhode Island and left the top down. Nick gazed at me with incredulity.

As we walked down the block to hail a cab, Nick had that brooding hunch to his shoulders. I remarked, rather gaily, "Oh, he has scads and scads of money."

"That's not the point."

I stopped and looked at him. "The point is I said I would take care of everything, didn't I?"

"I didn't expect you would tell a lie," he stated simply and flatly and I could tell that this incident had added a further difficult and complex layer to our relationship. He looked like a young Benjamin Franklin standing on the sidewalk, pen in hand to mark off how well he had done with his virtues for the day.

"I wouldn't call it a lie," I retorted, "—necessarily."

"Well, then, what *would* you call it?"

"Hedging my bets."

Nick laughed. "Amazing. Hedging my bets."

I saw something float into his eyes, not only that naïve, Mid-West, Boy Scout mentality, but also something cunning and challenging. I have never like men who thought themselves too clever or too shrewd because they then become too boring, and I hoped that this conversation would not ruin the fun that Nick and I had been having. That a hazard to avoid, a trap to escape, an obstacle to overcome. I knew he must have been thinking about that golf-ball-moving incident a couple of years ago—that has hounded my career, in one form or another, ever since, and I wished that it had never happened. But it did happen, and it's best to forget it.

Nick seems to want the world divided into good and bad, honest and dishonest, white and black, when the world is not so easily cut up and parceled out according to some patrician Christian index of sin. I will not be judged by some arbitrary code of conduct. Didn't Nick realize that the Great War had tossed out all those old, stale, fusty codes of morality?

"I live my life like jazz," I declared.

"And how is that?

"I improvise."

Aunt Sig adored Nick.

We were sitting and taking tea in her front parlor, a dark crowded Victorian room, all doilies and dust and antimacassars and heavy mahogany furniture, while Aunt Sig recounted a few historical moments in the Suffragist movement.

"Ah, yes, that was an afternoon in May," she said. "Terrible weather. Rain and drizzle all day. That was in 1910. We were such a motley crew, young and old, waving flags, carrying banners. All those hobble-skirted matrons shouting for justice. Do you remember those hobble skirts, dear? An utterly ridiculous fashion. But down Fifth Avenue we marched, and we hobbled demanding our right to vote. The cold rain and the constant jeering dampened the spirits of some marchers, who just dropped out. The parade was rather a fizzle, all in all, but we did make a statement. Ah, yes, those were some exciting days."

She sighed and sipped her tea, but her eyes snapped as she set her cup back in its saucer. "But we *did* win. I'm glad I lived long enough to see *that*."

Aunt Sig was in her late seventies or early eighties or mid-eighties—no one knew exactly how old she was and no one seemed to know how to find out. She was forgetful now, frail and feeble and sleepy, but when her mind was sharp, it was sharp. She sat there primly, a small, thin, unassuming woman in a simple white blouse and long dark skirt who did not so much wear her clothes as that her clothes wore her. It always amazed me that this tiny person had given speeches, had shouted in the streets, had been handcuffed and arrested.

"Did you wear yellow, Aunt Sig?" Nick asked.

She smiled. "I always wore a corsage of buttercups and jonquils. That way I could even *smell* our movement."

Nick laughed lightly.

"I must admit, my dear man," Aunt Sig whispered, "that I wept, like a silly young thing, the day Congress passed the Nineteenth

Amendment. June 4, 1919. I can die in peace now. My life has had meaning."

I felt instant pride for Aunt Sig. Her life *has* had meaning. She knew what to laugh at, as she always said, and laugh she did: at her husbands, at her family, at her society. She accomplished what she set out to do. And is that the meaning of a life? To set a goal and reach it? To choose one particular object or target or prize or cause, and devote your entire life to its attainment? It seemed too simple, and life is not that simple. And there are so many objects, targets, prizes, causes. What if you choose the wrong one?

Nick and I had started to talk about marriage.

"Ah, yes," Aunt Sig sighed. "Three husbands. I divorced twice."

"Is marriage a likely goal?" Nick asked.

"I'm not so sure about the future of the marriage institution," she went on, sighing and sipping her tea. "It might change for the better now that we are no longer seen as mere chattel! I don't know. I don't know what could possibly replace it. But it cannot remain as it always has been—this male trafficking in women. Oh, it's always been a ridiculous rivalry. No. It will change ... somehow change. That is for your generation to decide. I have done my work."

"Free love then," Nick suggested.

Aunt Sig considered this. "Perhaps. But I would think not *too* free."

Nick smiled broadly at this response and glanced at me.

Chapter V

"The tablecloths are so white," I remarked, apropos of nothing, as I sat down before our table in the tea garden of the Plaza Hotel.

Nick pushed my chair in, looked about abstractedly, and murmured some word of agreement.

"Even the napkins are so white," I continued, peering down at mine, shaped like some strange exotic flower, before flapping it out and placing it on my lap.

Nick sat down opposite me.

I asked, "So ... you had lunch with Gatsby?"

"I did."

He removed his napkin, shook it out, and placed it on his lap without another word. We didn't talk much, just idle chitchat about the weather and whatnot, until the waiter set down our teapot and watercress sandwiches on the table.

The waiter poured our tea. "The very best Earl Grey."

"Thank you," I said.

I pinched the corner of my sandwich and ate it. I could tell something was troubling him because he had that brooding hunch again. What had Gatsby told him? Probably not much. My role in this extraordinary affair was that of providing information, explaining situations, encouraging connections. I began to feel like some character in an Agatha Christie novel. Nick probably resents my being involved in some mystery attached to Gatsby since that makes *me* mysterious.

I moved the vase with the single red rose in it to the side (and remembered that ridiculous comment that Daisy had made), so I could have an unobstructed view of Nick to watch his reactions. I knew that our conversation this afternoon could change the shape of the entire summer ... or more. I had been dizzy with excitement after Gatsby sent me a telegram to say I could talk to Nick about what sad thing had happened to him and to ask Nick if he could arrange tea with Daisy at his cottage.

"And how was lunch?" I asked and sipped my tea.

"I met Mr. Wolfsheim," he said, but the name meant nothing to me.

"And who is Mr. Wolfsheim?" I asked.

Nick made some dismissive gesture with his hand. "One of Gatsby's 'business connegtions.'"

I squinted at him. "What's that again?"

"Oh, nothing, nothing, just someone Gatsby knows."

I sipped my tea and watched Nick.

"There were Presbyterian nymphs on the ceiling," he said.

"Oh," I said. "Forty-Second Street?"

"You know the place?"

"I know the place."

"You know quite a bit, don't you?"

"I try to know as much as I can," I replied in a straight voice. "That way you can make the best decisions."

"Or the worst choices," Nick remarked and then fell silent.

After a moment I asked, "Are you going to have some tea?"

"I don't care for any tea," Nick said forcefully. "I'd like to know what you and Gatsby have cooked up. And why do *you* have to talk to me and not him?"

"I didn't 'cook up' anything," I answered coolly. "And when you hear what I have to say, you'll understand better why I can tell you about it and not him."

"What is it then?"

"I was there," I said simply.

"There?"

"When Gatsby and Daisy first met."

Nick puzzled his brow.

"Do you remember," I asked, "when Gatsby and I talked in the library that night?"

“Of course, I do,” Nick said. “How could I forget that? But, as you said, you weren’t to tell anyone, and I didn’t bring up the matter at all since then.”

“You didn’t,” I said, and I liked Nick much more at that moment. “You were a good boy for not doing so. Are you always that good?”

“I try to be.”

“That shows you can keep promises. And you have more promises to keep before the afternoon is over.”

“I don’t like that,” Nick remarked. “I don’t like all this mystery and collusion. What is it? Just tell me.”

“I will,” I replied, sipped my tea, and set my teacup down. “Brace yourself.”

“I’ve been braced ever since I’ve come to this place. In fact, I’ve been learning to brace myself even when I don’t think I need to be braced.”

I laughed lightly and pouted slightly. “Nick, let’s not have a bum time.”

He didn’t respond.

“You know that Daisy and I grew up together.”

“In Louisville, of course,” he said and, with a mischievous tilt to his head, imitated Daisy’s voice, “Our beautiful white girlhood was passed there.”

I laughed at Nick and he laughed, too, and we both relaxed at that moment. Something tipped over inside me—the intrigue, the sharing, the involvement in this entanglement—that softened my attitude toward Nick.

"Well," I began and sat up straighter. "One day in October, in 1917, I was walking along from one place to another, half on the sidewalks, half on the lawns. I was happier on the lawns because I had these new shoes from England that had rubber nobs on the soles that bit into the soft ground."

"You always did have a lovely walk, Jordan. You *always* walk as though you have rubber nobs on the soles of your shoes, always biting into soft ground"—he smiled slightly as a memory drifted into his eyes—"I noticed that walk of yours at Gatsby's party. In fact, the thought occurred to me when you went off to have that talk with him."

I smiled back at him. "So you like the way I walk?"

"I do," Nick replied. "Very much."

"Anyway, I also had on a new plaid skirt that blew a little in the wind and whenever that happened the red, white, and blue banners in front of all the houses stretched out stiff and said *tut-tut-tut* in a disapproving way."

"*Tut-tut-tut.*"

"Really now, Nick." I giggled. "Will I ever be able to tell you this entire story or not?"

"Go on, go on."

"Well, the largest of the banners and the largest of the lawns, of course, belonged to Daisy Fay's house. She was just 18—I was 16—and she was by far the most popular young girl in all Louisville. She dressed in white and had a little white roadster and all day long the telephone rang in her house and excited young officers from Camp Taylor demanded the privilege of monopolizing her that night: 'anyways of an hour!'"

"For an hour!" Nick repeated. "Is that all?"

"Just to see Daisy—even for an hour—meant the world to some of those boys."

"She was *that* popular?"

"Oh, she was even more popular than that. When I came opposite her house that morning, her white roadster was beside the curb, and she was sitting in it with some lieutenant I had never seen before—I had become rather good at recognizing insignias and uniforms. The two of them were so engrossed in each other that she didn't even see me until I was five feet away. 'Hello, Jordan,' she called unexpectedly. 'Please come here.' I was flattered she wanted to speak to me because of all the older girls I admired her the most. She asked if I were going to the Red Cross to make bandages."

"Ah, to help save the world for democracy. To aid and abet the war to end wars."

"That's right. I was quite the patriotic girl. Well, she said, would I tell them that she couldn't come that day? I said of course I would. The officer gazed at Daisy while she was speaking, in a way that every young girl hopes to be looked at some time, and because it seemed so romantic to me, I have remembered that incident ever since."

"And I'm sure you've been looked at that way since then," Nick offered.

"And that has nothing to do with this story," I replied, smiling.

Nick chuckled. "Okay, go on."

"That lieutenant's name was Jay Gatsby, and I didn't lay eyes on him again for over four years—even after I'd met him a couple of times on Long Island I didn't realize it was the same man."

"You must be kidding me?" Nick said. "How could you *not* recognize him?"

"Well, I only saw him that one afternoon in Daisy's car and I didn't stare at him. Daisy had so many men coming over to her house or driving around in her little white roadster that I just added that lieutenant along with all the others, despite the love-lorn look he had in his eyes."

Comprehension began to bloom in Nick's eyes. "So Gatsby courted Daisy in Louisville ... the most popular girl in town."

I nodded.

"He was in love with her?"

"Oh, Nick, *everyone* was in love with her. That hardly mattered at the time. It was a desperate time, and these young boys were going overseas to war ... to be killed possibly. Can you really be critical of desperate affection?"

Nick shook his head in agreement. "Then what?"

"As I said, that was 1917. By the next year I had a few beaux myself, and I began to play in tournaments, so I didn't see Daisy very often. She went with a slightly older crowd—when she went with anyone at all."

"And how many beaux did Miss Baker have that year?"

"That is none of your business, Mr. Carraway."

Nick pouted, humorously, and something tipped over inside me again. It's odd how some type of intrigue can bewitch people and pull them together in unsuspected ways.

"Well, wild rumors," I continued, "were circulating about her—how her mother found her one winter night packing her suitcase to go to New York to say goodbye to a soldier who was going overseas."

"And that was ..."

"Who else could it be?"

"She was stopped, of course, but she didn't speak to her family for several weeks. After that, she didn't pal around with the soldiers anymore, only a few flat-footed, shortsighted young men in town who couldn't get into the army at all. Sad stray birds."

"Dates with the 4-F," Nick said. "Sounds like the title of a short story by Dorothy Parker."

"By next autumn, however, she was gay again—gay as ever. She had a début after the Armistice, and in February she was supposedly engaged to some man from New Orleans."

"New Orleans?" Nick asked. "Someone with Creole spice?"

I laughed softly. "All paprika and cayenne pepper. But in June she married Mr. Thomas Buchanan of Chicago with more pomp and circumstance than Louisville had ever known before."

"That's Tom. Reckless with money."

"Reckless with life," I added. "He came down with a hundred people in four private train cars and hired a whole floor of the Seelbach Hotel. The day before the wedding he gave Daisy a string of pearls valued at $350,000."

Nick whistled at the price of the pearls and made a kind of hangman's noose with his fingers about his neck. "What kind of girl could resist such a gift?"

I smiled beguilingly at him and did not answer.

"Oh," he said, "I see. You're not that kind of girl."

"Strings of pearls do not dazzle me."

"What does dazzle you, Jordan?"

Again I did not answer.

After that pause I continued. "I was a bridesmaid for the wedding, and half an hour before the bridal dinner, I went to her room and found her lying on her bed as lovely as the June night in a flowered dress—and as drunk as a monkey. She had a bottle of sauterne in one hand and a letter in the other.

"'Gratulate me,' she muttered. 'Never had a drink before but oh, how I do enjoy it.'

'What's the matter, Daisy?'

I was scared, I can tell you; I'd never seen her like that before.

'Here, dearis.' She groped around in a wastebasket she had with her on the bed and pulled out the string of pearls. 'Take 'em downstairs and give 'em back to whoever they belong to. Tell 'em all Daisy's change' her mine. Say 'Daisy's change' her mine!'"

Nick watched me in fascination, seeing his lovely cousin in a new light, a bold statement on their marriage and Daisy's frustration and indecision.

"She began to cry—she cried and cried. I rushed out and found her mother's maid and we locked the door and got her into a cold bath. She wouldn't let go of that letter. She took it into the tub with her and squeezed it up into a wet ball and only let me leave it in the soap dish when she saw it was coming to pieces like snow."

"Whatever happened to that letter?"

I shrugged. "I doubt it survived that bath."

"Whose letter was it? That man in New Orleans?"

I stared openly at Nick, somewhat dumbfounded at his lack of insight. "Who do you think?"

Then it struck him. "Of course."

"Nick. Of course. Of course of course. But Daisy didn't say another word. We gave her spirits of ammonia and put ice on her forehead and hooked her back into her dress. Half an hour later we walked out of that room with the pearls around her neck—the incident was over. The next day, at five o'clock, she married Tom without so much as a shiver and started off on a three months' trip to the South Seas."

"A string of pearls and a string of islands."

"And a string of lies and betrayals," I added with more emphasis than I intended.

Nick's eyes blinked. "What do you mean?"

"I saw them in Santa Barbara when they came back and I thought I'd never seen a girl so mad about her husband. If he left the room for a minute, she'd look around uneasily and say, 'Where's Tom gone?' and wear the most abstracted expression until she saw him coming in the door. She used to sit on the sand with his head in her lap by the hour rubbing her fingers through his hair, looking at him with unfathomable delight. It was touching to see them together—it made me laugh in a hushed, fascinated way. That was in August. A week after I left Santa Barbara, Tom ran into a wagon on Ventura Road one night and ripped a front wheel off his car. The girl who was with him got into the papers too because her arm was broken—she was one of the chambermaids in the Santa Barbara Hotel."

Nick simply shook his head.

"The next April Daisy had her little girl, and they went to France for a year. I saw them one spring in Cannes and later in Deauville and then they came back to Chicago to settle down."

"Did Pammy have any effect on their marriage?"

"What do you think, Nick?" I asked, with some anger edging my voice. Does he merely ask rhetorical questions or is he truly that dense. "You see how good a mother Daisy is, don't you? Or Tom as a father?"

Nick's expression seemed to sag.

"Didn't Daisy tell you what she said when Pammy was born?" I asked.

He nodded.

"And where was Tom *that* night?"

"Okay."

"Okay then. Daisy was popular in Chicago, you know. They moved with a fast crowd, all of them young and rich and wild, but she came out with an absolutely perfect reputation. Perhaps because she doesn't drink. It's a great advantage not to drink among hard-drinking people. You can hold your tongue and, moreover, you can time any little irregularity of your own so that everybody else is so blind that they don't see or care. Perhaps Daisy never went in for amour at all ... and yet there's something in that voice of hers ..."

"Yes," Nick agreed. "Her voice ... it's musical and slightly hushed ... you follow it up and down as if her voice were an arrangement of notes that will never be played again."

I ignored his remark, but Daisy does have a musical voice. "Well, about six weeks ago, she heard the name 'Gatsby' for the first time in years. At the dinner party when I first met you."

"I remember," Nick said. "I actually saw Gatsby later that night. Did I tell you?"

"No."

"After I came home," Nick explained, "after I ran the car under its shed, I sat for a while on an abandoned grass roller in the yard. All that talk about Tom's girl and Daisy's talk about how she's gotten to feel about 'things' and that everything was rotten ... I had a lot to think about. The wind was high and when I watched a cat moving in the moonlight, I followed it and then saw Gatsby emerge from the shadows of his mansion, standing with his hands in his pockets watching the sky. I was going to call to him. Just to introduce myself. As a neighbor. Since you mentioned him at dinner, I thought that would be sufficient for an introduction. But I never did call to him that night. I sensed he wanted to be alone ... and then ... then he stretched his arms out toward the water in a curious way. I glanced out at the water and saw nothing but a single green light, minute and far away—the light of a dock. Then he was gone."

I listened to this with grave interest. "Well, about the time you were seeing Gatsby that night, Daisy came up to my room and woke me to ask me about this Gatsby. I was half-asleep if not entirely asleep—I sometimes think I do things and say things when I *am* completely asleep—and I described him to her and she said it must be the man she used to know. I didn't know where she might have known him until it suddenly occurred to me that Gatsby was that young lieutenant with her in her white roadster."

The waiter appeared. We hadn't touched our sandwiches, except for that one lone corner I had pinched and ate.

"The check, please," Nick said.

On the sidewalk in front of the Plaza Hotel, I turned to Nick and said, "I haven't even told you yet what Gatsby wants."

"Let's take a ride through Central Park."

Half an hour later we were riding a Victoria through Central Park. The clip-clop of the horse's hooves sounded on the road and the gentle rocking motion of the carriage made me feel languorous and contented. The sun had disappeared behind the apartment building, and the sweet sounds of voices, little girls singing, harmonized with the clip-clopping hooves.

I'm the Sheik of Araby,
Your love belongs to me.

At night when you're asleep,
Into your tent I'll creep—

"It was a strange coincidence," Nick said about Gatsby's mansion.

"But it wasn't a coincidence at all."

"It wasn't?"

"Gatsby bought that house so that Daisy would be just across the Bay."

Nick's expression changed so suddenly that I repeated the words: "So that Daisy would be just across the Bay."

Obsessions are such a durable form. Nick gazed at the apartment buildings, at the reddish glow outlining the contours of the roofs, of the water towers.

"He wants to know—" I continued, quietly, "—if you'll invite Daisy to your house some afternoon for tea and then let him come over."

Nick's expression changed once again into one of amazement. "Did I have to know all this before he could ask such a little thing?"

"He's afraid. He's waited so long. He thought you might be offended. You see he's a regular tough underneath it all."

Nick turned to me with an odd look on his face now. "Why didn't he ask you to arrange a meeting in New York?

"He wants her to see his house," I explained. "And your house is right next door."

"Oh."

"I think he expected her to wander into one of his parties, some night, but she never did. He began asking people casually if they knew her, and I was the first one he found. It was that night he sent for me at his party, and you should have seen the elaborate way he worked up to it. Of course, I immediately suggested a luncheon in New York—and I thought he'd go mad: 'I don't want to do anything out of the way!' he kept saying. 'I want to see her right next door.' When I said you were a particular friend of Tom's, he started to abandon the whole idea. He doesn't know very much about Tom, though he says he's read a Chicago paper for years just on the chance of catching a glimpse of Daisy's name."

Nick didn't seem to be listening all that closely anymore, pursuing his own thoughts. Darkness had settled over the park as the Victoria dipped under a little bridge. Nick placed his arm around my shoulder, gently, and drew me toward him.

"Would you like to go to dinner tonight?" he asked.

The tone of his voice had shifted slightly. All this mysterious and machinating talk of Daisy and Gatsby must have had some effect on him. I leaned into him. Nick is fun. This can be fun, but I can't expect too much. I don't ever expect too much, but I can expect something.

"And Daisy," I murmured, "ought to have something in her life."

"Does she want to see Gatsby?"

"She's not to know about it. Gatsby doesn't want her to know. You're supposed to invite her to tea."

And then she will just be there. And then Gatsby will just be there. Gatsby was so fearful that she would refuse an agreed-upon meeting, but a chance meeting is entirely different. He's convinced that she'll be responsive to the situation ... to him. Daisy needs a little romance in her life. We all do, I suppose, of some kind—some kind of romance or affection or intimacy.

We passed a stand of thick, dark trees, and then the block of 59th Street, with its pale light that seemed like silver ribbons floating in the night. The carriage swayed and shook and the hooves clip-clopped and Nick abruptly drew me up next to him, his arms tight around me.

I smiled as he drew me up toward him, toward his face. Something, once again, tipped over inside me.

Chapter VI

Has it ever been this hot before? Whoever thought you would find the Delta along the Long Island Sound. Thank God for awnings and fans and iced drinks, but it was still so damnably hot that I didn't even want to *think*, nonetheless move from that enormous white couch. Daisy and I were in our usual positions. She was lying opposite me, all powdered and all dressed again in white, looking so much like a wilted magnolia blossom or some foolish odalisque waiting for her sheik.

Well, at least Daisy has something in her life now—but what will she do with it? Is that why we're here? She had been agitated all morning with this inscrutable look painted on her face. Everything about her seemed to falter and jerk. Gay one moment and then, not sad really, but blue and nervous.

Actually, I hadn't seen her too often this past month. I know she goes over to see Gatsby almost every day now, disappearing into that mansion, but she hasn't been all that much of a confidante. Although I have never had much interest in the sexual lives of other people (too many physical details about grunting specificity simple bore me), I do thrill to the details about the emotional complications and social configurations. I had to listen *ad naseum* to her whining about Tom and his girl in New York, so I felt a little miffed that she didn't confide the particulars about her long-lost lieutenant.

I heard the car in the drive.

And the telephone rang. That infernal machine, breathing disembodied voices into your life in various rooms and houses and hotels. "Yes ... yes ... I'll see." Then the footsteps. "Madam expects you in the salon!" That poor butler. His voice sounded hot. Even his footsteps sounded hot.

When we saw Nick and Gatsby in the doorway, we both called from our perches on the couch: "We can't move!"

Nick came over to me. I smiled and lifted my hand to his and let him hold my powdered fingers for a moment.

Nick straightened. "And where is Mr. Thomas Buchanan, the athlete?"

I noticed a perceptible twitch in Daisy's eyes, not a blink, but a twitch. Gatsby stiffened. Then I heard Tom's voice at the hall telephone. Gatsby stood in the middle of the crimson carpet, looking about the room with befuddled fascination. He was wearing his absurd pink suit, and I wondered idly what British tailor sewed together the outfit. Daisy watched him closely as he stood in the middle of the room and then laughed ... laughed that sweet silly dismissive laugh of hers as a tiny gust of powder rose from her bosom into the air like some stage effect.

"The rumor is," I whispered, "that that's Tom's girl on the telephone. Again."

I couldn't help making the remark. It was true. I'm a truthful and terribly honest girl. Every time I'm here it seems that woman calls at the most inopportune occasion.

Everyone fell silent.

We could hear Tom's deep voice rise in shrill annoyance. "Very well then, I won't sell you the car at all ... I'm under no obligations to you at all ... And as for your bothering me about it at lunch I won't stand that at all!"

"Holding down the receiver," Daisy said with cool cynicism.

That bad girl.

"No, he's not," Nick said. "It's a bona fide deal. I happen to know about it."

How would Nick know about that? Then Tom strode into the room.

"Mr. Gatsby!" Tom fairly shouted his name, extending his hand. "I'm glad to see you, sir ... Nick ..."

Oh, very glad indeed. Now, *this* is my idea of a house party.

"Make us a cold drink," Daisy commanded.

As soon as Tom left the room, Daisy stood up, went straight to Gatsby, pulled his face down to hers, and kissed him full on the mouth. Well, well.

"You know I love you," she said softly.

"You forget there's a lady present," I said.

Daisy looked around the room with exaggerated doubt on her face: where, where is the lady? The silly bitch.

"You kiss Nick too."

"What a low, vulgar girl!" I cried, with some embarrassment.

"I don't care!" Daisy cried and then, astonishingly, she stared to dance a clog on the hearth of the brick fireplace. In this heat. She stopped as suddenly as she began and dropped back down on the couch just as a nurse led Pammy into the room.

"Bles-sed pre-cious," she crooned and held out her arms. "Come to your own mother that loves you."

Pammy hurried across the room and buried herself in Daisy's lap.

"The Bles-sed pre-cious! Did mother get powder on your old yellow hair? Stand up now and How-de-do."

Such a show. Pammy politely extended her hand to both Nick and Gatsby. Gatsby had this extraordinarily incomprehensible expression on his face, staring at the child. Did he think Pammy didn't exist? That Daisy and Tom made her up for the sake of appearances?

"I got dressed before luncheon," Pammy said, turning back to her mother.

"That's because your mother wanted to show you off." Daisy bent her face into the girl's neck. "You dream, you. You absolute little dream.'

"Yes," Pammy agreed, with a touch of hesitation. "Aunt Jordan's got on a white dress too."

I smiled at her.

"How do you like mother's friends?" Daisy asked, turning Pammy to face Gatsby again. "Do you think they're pretty?"

"Where's Daddy?"

That's a logical question.

"She doesn't look like her father," Daisy remarked. "She looks like me. She's got my hair and shape of the face."

And you hope that she'll become a beautiful little fool.

The nurse called to Pammy, "Come, Pammy," as though we were some groomed poodle, trained to perform tricks for the guests.

"Goodbye, sweetheart!"

Oh, yes, hello, spin around I-love-you-my-precious-blessed, goodbye. The poor child glanced back at all of us with an innocent longing, but docilely held her hand out to the nurse and disappeared.

Tom returned with four gin rickeys, the glasses jammed with crushed ice.

Gatsby took his drink and remarked, in a tense voice, "They certainly look cool."

We all drank the cool drinks with sticky greediness.

"I read somewhere that the sun's getting hotter every year," Tom said in his scientific voice. "It seems that pretty soon the earth's going to fall into the sun—or wait a minute—it's just the opposite—the sun's getting colder every year."

Some new book he's been reading.

"Come outside," Tom said to Gatsby. "I'd like you to have a look at the place."

And there goes the Demaine-the-oil-man routine as the men exited the room. This might prove to be a duller afternoon than I realized.

Finally, we sat down to luncheon in the darkened dining room. The entire house was dark against the heat. I could hardly eat anything at all but drank down my cold ale with delicious relief.

"What'll we do with ourselves this afternoon," Daisy said, "and the day after that, and the next thirty years?"

"Don't be morbid," I said. "Life starts all over again when it gets crisp in the fall."

"But it's so hot," Daisy remarked, her eyes literally tearful. "And everything's so confused. Let's all go to town!"

Is everything confused? I heard steps again as Tom and Gatsby returned to join us at the table.

Tom said to Gatsby, "I've heard of making a garage out of a stable, but I'm the first man who ever made a stable out of a garage."

Tom is sometimes such a perfect bore.

"Who wants to go the town?" Daisy insisted.

I watched as Gatsby's eyes drifted from Tom to Daisy.

"Ah," she said to him, "you look so cool."

Their eyes meshed. Unbelievably, they just sat staring at each other across the table as if no one else were in the dining room. Then Daisy, with visible effort, broke her gaze and glanced down at her plate and fork.

"You always look so cool," she repeated.

Tom was dumbfounded, his mouth literally open. He looked at Gatsby and then back at Daisy with this astonished expression etched into his face. Should he be so surprised when his girl rings up at lunch and dinner and all hours of the day? Tom. Men. So the table turns. Positively amusing.

"You resemble the advertisement of the man," Daisy went on. "You know the advertisement of the man—"

"All right," Tom barked. "I'm perfectly willing to go to town. Come on—we're all going to town."

He stood up, his eyes flashing and snapping all the while from Daisy to Gatsby and Gatsby to Daisy. All the rest of us just remained silent.

"Come on!" Tom's temper cracked a little. "What's the matter anyhow? If we're going to town, let's start."

Tom was using all he had to control himself. His hand trembled slightly as he finished his ale. When Daisy spoke, we all stood and moved out to the driveway.

"Are we just going to go?" she said. "Like this? Aren't we going to let anyone smoke a cigarette first?"

"Everybody smoked all through dinner," Tom declared.

"Oh, let's have fun," Daisy implored. "It's too hot to fuss."

Too hot to fuss. Yes, let's postpone the topic of adultery for the moment because the temperature is in the 90s. Tom did not answer.

"Have it your way," she hissed. "Come on, Jordan."

Oh, yes, Jordan. The ladies will retire for a moment to powder their noses ... their silver noses ... if you please. I followed Daisy, who walked with a determined, defiant step into the house.

After we climbed the stairs and reached the second floor, Daisy turned to me. "It's this house, Jordan. It's this house."

"What are you talking about?"

"We can't be the same in this house."

"Which 'we' are we talking about?"

Daisy's beautiful blue eyes flashed with anger for a moment before settling with a flutter of mischief on my face. "Oh, that's why I love to have you around, Jordan. I really do." And with that remark, she laughed and flounced off to her room.

I stepped down to my room, since I was spending the weekend here—Daisy had insisted, and I wondered now what her true motive was for doing so. I sensed that something momentous or irrevocable was about to happen in this household. Was I to be a witness? A support?

I did powder my nose and gathered up some traveling accessories. In the foyer we met Tom, who was wrapping a quart bottle of whiskey in a white towel. Daisy and I had both pulled on small tight metallic cloth hats on our heads, which were all the rage that season, and carried light capes over our arms. As we followed Tom back outside, the heat dropped on us. The day was virtually white. White and hot and sticky.

"Shall we all go in my car?" Gatsby asked, leaning into the car to feel the green leather seat. "I ought to have left it in the shade."

"Is it a standard shift?" Tom asked.

"Yes."

"Well, you take my coupé and let me drive your car to town."

The suggestion of switching cars, which was just a lark on Tom's part, clearly discomposed Gatsby. "I don't think there's much gas."

"Plenty of gas," Tom said with boisterous good spirits as he looked in at the gauge. "And if it runs out, I can stop at a drug store. You can buy anything at a drug store nowadays."

Another of Tom's *non-sequiturs*. Or was it? I watched some glimmer of intelligence and challenge shine in Tom's eyes. Daisy frowned. Nick gazed innocently at Tom, as though he were used to these cryptic remarks, but Gatsby's expression flickered slightly from surprise to wariness.

"Come on, Daisy," Tom insisted and tried moving her toward the car. "I'll take you in this circus wagon."

As he opened the door to Gatsby's car, Daisy slipped from him. "You take Nick and Jordan. We'll follow you in the coupé."

She hurried back to Gatsby then, touching the edge of his pink suit coat. How in the world will this all play itself out? All this posturing and posing. I slid into the front seat and Nick slid in next to me. Tom pushed and shoved the gears and we shot off, with a violent jerk, into the white heavy sticky heat.

"Did you see that?" Tom snarled.

"See what?" Nick asked.

My poor dear Nick. I glanced over at him. Perhaps he really didn't see.

Tom looked at him briefly with sharp eyes. "You think I'm pretty dumb, don't you? Perhaps I am, but I have a—almost a second sight, sometimes, that tells me what to do.

Maybe you don't believe that, but science—" He stopped his little speech abruptly, paused, and decided, I suppose, that science would not help him with this situation. "I've made a small investigation of this fellow. I could have gone deeper if I'd known—"

"Do you mean you've been to a medium?" I asked, amazed at his shenanigans—that he would need to investigate and interrogate.

"What?" he said, confused, as Nick and I both laughed. "A medium?"

"About Gatsby," I said.

"About Gatsby! No, I haven't. I said I'd been making a small investigation of his past."

"And you found he was an Oxford man," I said, trying to help him. He's getting all caught up in the rumors about Gatsby, though he's about two months too late. That was the game at the start of the summer, but it's not the game now.

"An Oxford man!" Tom snorted. "Like hell he is! He wears a pink suit."

"Nevertheless, he's an Oxford man," Nick said.

"Oxford, New Mexico," Tom remarked contemptuously, "or something like that."

Annoyed at this last comment, I asked, "Listen, Tom, if you're such a snob, why did you invite him to lunch?"

"Daisy invited him; she knew him before we were married—God knows where!"

I glanced at Nick, who shook his head slightly and returned his gaze to the road before us. We were all hot and sticky and annoyed at this point, and silence seemed the best method of communication. When that huge billboard of faded eyes came into sight, Nick turned to Tom and reminded him about the gasoline.

"We've got enough to get us to town," Tom said.

"But there's a garage right here," I said. "I don't want to get stalled in traffic in this baking heat."

Abruptly, Tom threw on both brakes. The car slid to a dust-tossed stop under the sign that said "Repairs. George B. Wilson. Cars Bought and Sold." I had seen this building every time I went out to Long Island, but I had never stopped at it before. One empty shop, one restaurant, one garage—all jammed into this single, sad-looking, yellow building.

This whole area was dismal and broken down. All ashes and waste. I thought back to that time Nick and I had been stopped by those trucks. A true hazard, I decided. In the distance stood that useless billboard with those pale-staring eyes. Those persistent staring eyes. I wished now that I had not made Tom stop when this shadow, it seemed, materialized in the doorway of the building.

"Let's have some gas!" Tom yelled. "What do you think we stopped for—to admire the view?"

"I'm sick," the man said, still standing in the doorway. "I been sick all day."

Nick moved restlessly, shifting his legs and turning to look at the man.

"What's the matter?" Tom asked, the annoyance dripping from his voice.

"I'm all run down."

"Well, shall I help myself? You sounded well enough on the phone."

Oh, so *this* was the man about the car. It *wasn't* Tom's girl on the telephone. The shadow-man moved into the hot afternoon light and, breathing stertorously, unscrewed the cap of the tank. He literally looked green in the sunlight.

"I didn't mean to interrupt your lunch," the green voice apologized. "But I need money pretty bad and I was wondering what you were going to do with your old car."

"How do like this one?" Tom asked. "Bought it last week."

Sometimes I do like Tom.

"It's a nice yellow one," Wilson said.

"Like to buy it?"

"Big chance. No, but I could make some money on the other."

"What do you want money for all of a sudden?"

"I've been here too long. I want to get away. My wife and I plan to go west."

"Your wife does!" Tom fairly shouted.

"She's been talking about it for ten years." The man rested against the pump for a moment, covering his eyes with his hand. "And now she's going whether she wants to or not. I'm going to get her away."

The bliss of marriage, I thought bitterly. At every level of society, the man dictates and shouts and beats down the woman. Just then, Tom's blue coupé flashed by in a flurry of dust. I saw Daisy give us a small wave.

"What do I owe you?" Tom said roughly.

"Dollar twenty."

Nick seemed so odd, watching this exchange between the green man and Tom.

"I'll let you have that car," Tom said. "I'll send it over tomorrow afternoon."

Nick kept looking about at the yellow building, as though he were expecting someone else to materialize out of the shadows.

"Just the eyes watching," I said.

"What?" Nick replied, looking at me.

"The eyes of Dr. Eckleburg," I said, indicating the billboard.

He stared at me a moment. "Yes, yes. Those eyes."

"Always watching us, Nick."

Tom slammed the car into gear and jerked away from the pump back onto the dusty road. He switched gears furiously as his mood switched into higher degrees of anger. Because I made him stop for gas? Bickering about cars?

We sped gloriously along Astoria at 50 miles per hour. The breeze was delicious. And what joy to see the New York skyline come into view. I knew Tom was trying to catch up with Gatsby and, pretty soon, we did, among the black lacy girders of the elevated.

"Those big movie houses around 50th Street are cool," I said. "I love New York on summer afternoons when everyone's away. There's something very sensuous about it—overripe, as if all sorts of funny fruits were going to fall into your hands."

Nick and Tom said nothing and then the blue coupé stopped with Daisy signaling to us to draw alongside.

"Where are we going?" she cried.

"How about the movies?" I called back.

"It's so hot," she whined. "You go. We'll ride around and meet you after. We'll meet you on some corner. I'll be the man smoking two cigarettes."

Just then a truck honked at us to move along.

"We can't argue about it here," Tom said. "You follow me to the south side of Central Park, in front of the Plaza."

As we drove there, Tom kept turning around and looking back at them to make sure Daisy and Gatsby were indeed following us. I don't know if he expected them to dart away on their own down some alley or pull some kind of stunt like that.

After parking the car and clambering out on the side, all I wanted to do was to get in some shade and sit under a whirring fan. With the sun spilling down and the hot concrete and the fact that my suggestion about the movies had been vetoed all made me feel a little surly, and when I feel surly, I need shade and a cold drink. Even on the fairway, I try to get in the shade when I get skittery and surly. Tom and Gatsby were talking at one point about how differently the cars performed. Men and their automobiles. A car drives, from point A to point B—that's it. I finally left the crowd on the sidewalk and walked into the lobby of the Plaza to get out of the heat.

"Jordan?" Nick was following me. "Jordan? Are you all right?"

"It's just the heat."

He nodded.

Soon everyone had crowded into the lobby while Daisy marched straight to the front desk with this officious old man standing there. Bellhops snapped to attention looking for our bags.

"We'd like ...," she looked around, "one, two, three, four ... five rooms. No five bathrooms, please, and lots of ice and cold water."

The old man, at first entranced by Daisy's beauty and that hushed voice of hers, gradually became un-entranced at her suggestion. "I'm afraid, madam, that we do not rent our bathrooms."

Daisy giggled. Gatsby laughed out right. Even Nick smiled. Tom stood there with a poker face. We all started talking at once then, until someone finally suggested that we rent a single suite to lounge in and cool off and have a mint julep.

The bellhop, with an odd look of incomprehension at the ways of the rich, opened the door to the suite. Tom gave him an oversized tip. Since we had no bags, the bellhop hopped away.

Tom strode into the room. He was back to striding. He opened the windows as the rest of us filed in. Removing her hat Daisy floated immediately over to a mirror on the far wall and started fixing her hair. Vanity, oh vanity. The room was large but stifling. No way to avoid the heat. Best to stay still. Simply remain still. Motionless.

"It's a swell suite," I said and dropped myself into an overstuffed chair.

Everyone laughed as though I had cracked a joke.

"Open another window," Daisy commanded, still staring into the mirror and patting at her hair.

"There aren't any more."

"Well, we'd better telephone for an axe—"

"The thing to do is to forget about the heat," Tom said. "You make it ten times worse by crabbing about it."

He unrolled the bottle of whiskey from the towel and set it on a table.

"Why not let her alone, old sport," Gatsby said. "You're the one what wanted to come to town."

Silence. The telephone book slipped from its nail and splashed onto the floor, pages opening.

"Excuse me," I said, but no one laughed at that.

"I'll pick it up," Nick said.

"I've got it," Gatsby said, examining the parted string, and said, "Hum!" in an odd way before tossing the book on a chair.

"That's a great expression of yours, isn't it?" Tom said sharply.

"What is?"

"All this 'old sport' business. Where'd you pick that up?"

"Now see here, Tom," Daisy said firmly, turning from the mirror, "if you're going to make personal remarks, I won't stay here a minute. Call up and order some ice for the mint julep."

Surprisingly, Tom picked up the receiver and, at that moment, the heat in the room burst into sound—the chords of Mendelssohn's *Wedding March* from the ballroom below.

"Imagine marrying anyone in this heat," I said dismally.

"Still—I was married in the middle of June," Daisy said. "Louisville in June! Somebody fainted. Who was it fainted, Tom?"

"Biloxi."

"A man name Biloxi. 'Blocks' Biloxi, and he made boxes—that's a fact—and he was from Biloxi, Tennessee."

"They carried him into my house," I added, "because we lived just two doors from the church. And he stayed three weeks, until Daddy told him he had to get out. The day after he left Daddy died." Everyone simply stared at me, and I thought I might have been irreverent. "There wasn't any connection," I added.

"I used to know a Bill Biloxi from Memphis," Nick then said, as through trying to move the conversation as far away from my last remark as possible.

"That was his cousin," I said. "I knew his whole family history before he left. He gave me an aluminum putter that I use today."

And I do. And it works well.

The music had died down during the ceremony and now a long cheer floated up into the window, followed by intermittent cries of "Yea—ea—ea!" and finally by a burst of jazz as the dancing began.

"We're getting old," Daisy said. "If we were young, we'd rise and dance."

The girl is 23 years old and thinks she's old. I'm 21. Daisy wants life to be a series of debutante balls. Always 18. Always 18.

"Remember Biloxi," I said. Dancing in this type of heat. "Where'd you know him, Tom?"

"Biloxi?" He concentrated. "I didn't know him. He was a friend of Daisy's."

"He was not," she claimed. "I'd never seen him before. He came down in the private car."

"Well, he said he knew you. He said he was raised in Louisville. Asa Bird brought him around at the last minute and asked if we had room for him."

I smiled. "He was probably bumming his way home. He told me he was president of your class at Yale."

Tom and Nick looked at each other with blank expressions.

"Biloxi?"

"First place, we didn't have any president—"

Gatsby's foot beat a series of restless taps. Tom turned to him abruptly and said, "By the way, Mr. Gatsby, I understand you're an Oxford man."

"Not exactly."

Hmm. I never did believe that, and now it comes out.

"Oh, yes, I understand you went to Oxford," Tom continued, almost as though he were a prosecutor in a court of moral law.

Gatsby paused.

Then Tom, his voice rising and shrill, said, "You must have gone there about the time Biloxi went to New Haven."

The implication was oh-so subtle. Tom and his strides. His voice assumed the same striding, stomping steps.

A pause again. Then a knock at the door. A waiter brought in some crushed mint and ice and a “thank you” when Tom tipped him. The pause, however, sat in the room as though someone else had joined our festive little overheated party.

“I told you I went there,” Gatsby said with challenge in his voice.

“I hear you, but I’d like to know when,” Tom demanded.

“It was in 1919. I only stayed five months. That’s why I can’t really call myself an Oxford man.”

Tom glanced around at all of us with a smug expression to see if we shared his disbelief.

“It was an opportunity they gave to some of the officers after the Armistice,” he continued. “We could go to any of the universities in England or France.”

So that was it. Nick seemed to beam with satisfaction. It looked as if he were going to slap Gatsby on the back and shake his hand in vigorous pumps. Gatsby, really, is a consummate liar, I thought. He tells the truth, but he doesn’t tell the truth. Or he provides the hint of truth without the whole truth. A man of semi-truths that lets rumors and mysteries surround him. I can admire a man like that.

Daisy, who sat and watched this entire dialogue, rose quietly and went to the table where the whiskey bottle sat with the ice and mint.

"Open the whiskey, Tom," she said. "And I'll make you a mint julep. Then you won't seem so stupid to yourself .... Look at the mint!"

Yes, look at the mint—that's a good diversionary tactic.

"Wait a minute," Tom snapped. "I want to ask Mr. Gatsby one more question."

"Go on," Gatsby responded in a polite tone.

"What kind of row are you trying to cause in my house anyhow?"

Here it comes. Tom won't let it go. Won't let go. He's standing there like some medieval knight having thrown down the gauntlet. And all the while he has his own girl somewhere blocks away. The hypocrisy is exquisite.

"He isn't causing a row," Daisy cried out, looking from one to the other. "You're causing a row. Please have a little self-control."

"Self-control!" Tom repeated loudly. "I suppose the latest thing is to sit back and let Mr. Nobody from Nowhere make love to your wife. Well, if that's the idea you can count me out.... Nowadays people begin by sneering at family life and family institutions and next they'll throw everything overboard and have intermarriage between black and white."

I thought Tom glanced at me when he said that. All of a sudden, Daisy's little afternoon trysts have become the revolutionary tactics of a dark-race cabal that will bring down the Nordic race. What ridiculous books does Tom keep reading?

"We're all white here," I murmured, keeping an edge of anger from my voice.

"I know I'm not very popular," Tom went on. "I don't give big parties. I suppose you've got to make your house into a pigsty in order to have any friends—in the modern world."

I could barely keep my contempt intact. If he thinks that not throwing parties is the reason he doesn't have any friends, then—

"I've got something else to tell *you*, old sport—" Gatsby interrupted my thought and then Daisy interrupted Gatsby.

"Please don't! Please let's all go home. Why don't we all go home?"

Home? Is that what it's called?

"That's a good idea," Nick agreed. "Come on, Tom. Nobody wants a drink."

And that's Nick for you as well: avoid confrontation.

"I want to know what Mr. Gatsby has to tell me," Tom said.

I certainly do if no one else does. I glanced at Daisy's pale face and then turned to Gatsby to hear what he has to say.

"Your wife doesn't love you," he said in a hushed voice. "She's never loved you. She loves me."

"You must be crazy!" Tom shouted.

We *all* must be crazy. Could he really be saying what he told me that night in his library? I stared at Gatsby in his pink suit and wondered if he had rehearsed those lines, those silly lines he must have plucked from a particularly bad romance story in the *Saturday Evening Post*. That's what this is—an Edginton serial or a Tristram Tupper short story.

Gatsby, as if on cue, sprang to his feet. "She never loved you, do you hear? She only married you because I was poor and she was tired of waiting for me. It was a terrible mistake, but in her heart she never loved anyone except me!"

Is it possible I'm hearing this? Who could say such trite things? Tom was overheating—he had switched into a higher gear, flushed and firm and angry. This was clearly not a place for a good girl like me. When I got up to go and noticed that Nick, too, had decided to leave, Gatsby insisted that we stay.

"Don't go," he said firmly. "That must be known."

I sat back down. Do I really have to witness this? Does Gatsby need an audience?

"Sit down, Daisy," Tom said, roughly but attempting to discover a quiet note in his voice.

"What's been going on? I want to hear all about it."

"I told you what's been going on," Gatsby declared. "Going on for five years—and you didn't know."

If it's been going on for five years and no one knew, then that's a mystery to me. And, I'm sure, to Daisy. I think this has been going on for five years in Mr. Jay Gatsby's overactive imagination and nowhere else.

Tom turned to Daisy. "You've been seeing this fellow for five years?"

Tom, for all his brutishness, at least attempts to sick to facts. Does he really think that Daisy has been having an affair for *five* years?

"Not seeing," Gatsby explained. "No, we couldn't meet. But both of us loved each other all that time, old sport, and you didn't know. I used to laugh sometimes to think that you didn't know."

"Oh—that's all."

That's all. Isn't this deliciously romantic? Imagine what Edgar Wallace could do with a sentiment like that.

"I can't speak about what happened five years ago because I didn't know Daisy then—" Tom continued, "and I'll be damned if I see how you got within a mile of her unless you brought the groceries to the back door. But all the rest of that's a God Damned lie. Daisy loved me when she married me and she loves me now."

"No," Gatsby said, shaking his head and placing all the romantic idealism he had in that single denial.

"She does, though," Tom went on. "The trouble is that sometimes she gets foolish ideas in her head and doesn't know what she's doing." He nodded knowingly. "And what's more, I love Daisy too. Once in a while I go off on a spree and make a fool of myself, but I always come back, and in my heart I love her all the time."

Now, Tom was doing it: the love talk. In my heart. All the time. And it was always okay for a man to have a "spree," but not a woman. Marriage! What an institution!

"You're revolting," Daisy interjected. "Do you know why we left Chicago?" She turned, not to me, but to Nick, because of course I knew and he didn't. "I'm surprised that they didn't treat you to the story of that little spree."

And that *was* quite a little spree, according to Daisy, but before she could say anything Gatsby stepped over and stood beside her.

"Daisy, that's all over now," he said. "It doesn't matter anymore. Just tell him the truth—that you never loved him—and it's all wiped out forever."

What was he saying? What did he want done?

"Why—" Daisy began, flustered and flushed. "—how could I love him—possibly?"

"You never loved him," Gatsby said, tightly and stubbornly, as though saying those four words would transform the reality of the world for everyone involved. He wanted to believe that she never loved anyone else then her love for him had never been tainted, somehow remaining pure and eternal. What possible good could become of that? What kind of delusional dream was he living in? Embracing?

Daisy hesitated. She looked at me and then at Nick with some sort of desperate appeal, as though she had forgotten her lines and we were prompters at the edge of a stage. I thought she only understood at that moment what was going on—the Wife and her Lover were confronting the Husband. She has been having an affair with a former fling. The former fling wanted the fling to be more than a fling. No spree here, I'm afraid ... or, rather, this will be a spree that could match and outdo any of Tom's sprees in the past.

"I never loved him," she murmured, with obvious reluctance—lines an actress was trying to learn but without context or motivation.

"Not at Kapiolani?" Tom said gently.

"No."

Music wafted upward again, or at least I became *aware* of music again, as if a sudden score were being played to accompany this absurd tragic scene.

"Not that day I carried you down from the Punch Bowl to keep your shoes dry? ... Daisy?"

"Please don't."

Tom seemed almost tender. Daisy, for all her initial coldness toward him, now seemed ... just empty. She looked pleadingly at Gatsby.

"There, Jay," she said and tried to light a cigarette, but her hand shook. Then, abruptly, she threw the cigarette and the burning match on the carpet. "Oh, you want too much! I love you now—isn't that enough? I can't help what's past." She began to sob. "I did love him once—but I loved you too."

Poor confused girl. A fool. A beautiful little fool. Isn't that it, Daisy?

Gatsby blinked, the way you blink when there's a light shone into your eyes. "You love me *too*?"

All the emphasis on that little word. Too.

"Even that's a lie," Tom came back with savagery. "She didn't know you were alive. Why ... there're things between Daisy and me that you'll never know, things that neither of us can ever forget."

Gatsby stood rigid. "I want to speak to Daisy alone. She's all excited now—"

"Even alone I can't say I never loved Tom," she said in a small, terribly honest voice. "It wouldn't be true."

The poor girl was all excited, Mr. Gatsby. The excitement must be the reason she can't say she never loved Tom—not the truth, not the reality.

"Of course, it wouldn't," Tom said.

Daisy turned to him. “As if it mattered to you.”

“Of course, it matters. I’m going to take better care of you from now on.”

I doubt it, but it might be true. If a husband saw his own behavior with his wife, would that change the man?

“You don’t understand,” Gatsby announced. “You’re not going to take care of her anymore.”

“I’m not?” Tom said and laughed. “Why’s that?”

“Daisy’s leaving you.’

“Nonsense.”

“I am, though,” she said with visible effort.

So *that’s* what this was all about—a divorce. Daisy decided to be positively amusing.

“She’s not leaving me!” Tom shouted. “Certainly not for a common swindler who’d have to steal the ring he put on her finger.”

“I won’t stand this!” Daisy shrieked. “Oh, please let’s get out.”

“Who are you anyhow?” Tom said, turning fiercely on Gatsby. “You’re one of that bunch that hangs around with Meyer Wolfsheim—that much I happen to know. I’ve made a little investigation into your affairs—and I’ll carry it further tomorrow.”

There’s that Wolfsheim name again. Must be the mob.

"You can suit yourself about that, old sport," Gatsby responded but unsteadily.

Men battling over their women. The barter. The trafficking. I guess the vote hadn't helped us out all that much.

"I found out what your 'drug stores' were," Tom declared and turned to the entire room to speak like a Pinkerton Detective. "He and this Wolfsheim bought up a lot of side-street drug stores here and in Chicago and sold grain alcohol over the counter. That's one of his little stunts. I picked him for a bootlegger the first time I saw him and I wasn't far wrong."

So Gatsby *is* a bootlegger. What else?

"What about it?" Gatsby replied coolly. "I guess your friend Walter Chase wasn't too proud to come in on it."

"And you left him in the lurch, didn't you? You let him go to jail for a month in New Jersey. God! You ought to hear Walter on the subject of *you*."

"He came to us dead broke. He was very glad to pick up some money, old sport."

"Don't you call me 'old sport'!" Tom yelled.

So the violence begins. All of Tom's talk about civilized races is up for bargain.

"Walter could have put you up on the betting laws too," Tom continued, his voice rising,
"but Wolfsheim scared him into shutting his mouth."

I looked at Gatsby and felt a shiver run along my skin. I could hear that girl in the yellow dress say, "Somebody told me they thought he killed a man once." I felt my chin rising.

"That drug store business was just small change," said Tom, "but you've got something on now that Walter's afraid to tell me about."

I looked at Daisy now, who sat with a frightened expression beaded on her face, glancing from Tom to Gatsby to Nick to me. Daisy needed something in her life. She needed this affair ... but was she up to an affair with a bootlegger, a criminal, a possible killer?

Gatsby started to talk to her. "None of this is true, Daisy, none of it, not the way Tom is describing it. You must believe me." Daisy's bright blue eyes had become tarnished. Tom, I knew at that exact moment, had shut the door on this affair. For all of Daisy's enthusiasm and excitement and tentative steps into unfamiliar territory, all this talk about bootlegging and illegal betting and jail would be too much for her proper white upbringing.

"*Please*, Tom! I can't stand this anymore."

The beautiful little fool. Whatever had she planned to do this afternoon was gone forever. Daisy's golf ball landed in the lake, lost to sight. Her handicap, at this point, was far too great, and she would lose this game.

"You two start on home, Daisy," Tom suggested. "In Mr. Gatsby's car."

Why would Tom suggest that? Some new scientific theory of psychology?

"Go on. He won't annoy you. I think he realizes that his presumptuous little flirtation is over."

Score. Hole in one. The affair was over—just like that.

After a moment, Tom began wrapping the unopened bottle of whiskey in the towel. We never did have our mint juleps. I gazed at the melting ice and the wilted sprigs of mint.

"Want any of this stuff? Jordan?"

I shook my head.

"Nick?"

He didn't answer.

"Nick?"

"What?"

"Want any?"

"No ... I just remembered that today's my birthday."

I looked over at Nick. "Well, Nick, happy birthday."

I don't remember exactly how we left the room or got down to the lobby, but we did. It was already past seven o'clock when we climbed into Tom's blue coupé and started the journey back to Long Island. I should have just signaled a taxi and gone straight to Aunt Sig's apartment, but I only thought of that later ... much later.

Tom moved boisterously—that striding step once again—and talked boisterously the entire time in the unmistakable tone of voice of one who has triumphed. I've heard that tone before with so many men and women on the circuit. It's a tone of practiced nonchalance that masks the excitement and pride of having won, definitely, a silver trophy.

I sat silent next to Nick and wondered what he would make of all this. Of all this nonsense and stuff. I had encouraged Daisy to have this affair. And why not? Some fun, some thrills. To have a little something in her life. But she shouldn't have had an affair with someone from her past—that had been the mistake. And Gatsby himself.

Filled with too much emotion and thoughts, I let my head lean against Nick's shoulder. I tried to figure out what was surging through that "honest" mind of his and took his hand as we crossed over the bridge back into the twilight of Long Island.

I had dozed off, actually, when Tom abruptly jerked into a lower gear.

"Wreck!" Tom shouted.

I blinked awake and stared through the windshield. I could see a few cars and a knot of people up ahead, near that dismal yellow building.

"That's good," Tom declared. "Wilson'll have a little business at last."

I shrugged and sat up straight, looking up the road, as Tom slowed down further.

I hoped he wouldn't stop. I wanted to get back to the house and to my room and to my bed. All this marital upheaval has been enough for me. When we neared the garage, however, he stopped the car.

"We'll take a look," he said, "just a look."

"Just a look," I echoed. Do men never cease to be fascinated by accidents and machinery and wrecks and wars? "I don't like this. I think we should just go home."

Tom pushed open his door and jumped out. Nick followed. I decided I didn't want to sit in the car alone, so I climbed out too and hurried after Nick. As we approached the crowd gathered near the garage, I heard a horrendous wailing sound that at first didn't even seem human—more like some siren.

"Oh My Ga-od!

"Oh My Ga-od!

"Oh My Ga-od!"

The single voice—a male voice—wailed those three words over and over and over.

"There's some bad trouble here," Tom said with excitement stirring his voice as we reached the outer wall of people slumped around that sad-looking building.

Tom stood on his tiptoes to peer into the garage and made a sudden harsh noise and with forcefulness elbowed and pushed his way past the standing gawking crowd. What's going on with Tom? I looked over at Nick, who was peering into the garage as well, intent upon the scene with a rather ugly attention. The crowd seemed to swallow Tom and then rearranged itself and somehow Nick and I were jostled to the front.

A woman lay wrapped in a blanket on a dirty worktable by the wall. And Tom, with his back to us, stood motionless next to her, bending over her. She was dead. What in the world happened? There's no wreck I can see.

Next to Tom stood a man and a motorcycle cop writing something into a small black book. I looked around the room, still hearing that wailing voice, and saw a man—the green man who spoke to Tom earlier, who filled the car with gasoline—swaying back and forth in his office holding the doorposts with both hands. "Oh My Ga-od!" Over and over. Another man right next to him was trying to comfort him. I looked back at Tom, who quickly jerked up and stared wildly about the room, as though he were searching for something.

"M-a-v—" the cop said, writing into his book, "—o—"

"No, —r—" the other man corrected. "M-a-v-r-o—"

"Listen to me!" Tom shouted.

"r—" said the cop. "o—"

"g—"

"g—"

Tom dropped his hand on the cop's shoulder who asked gruffly, "What you want, fella?"

"What happened—that's what I want to know!"

"Auto hit her. Ins'antly killed."

"Instantly killed," Tom repeated, staring off at nothing.

"She ran out ina road. Son-of-a-bitch didn't even stopus car."

A hit and run. Hit and run. But what's wrong with Tom?

"There was two cars," said another man. His name was Michaelis, I think. "One comin', one goin', see?"

"Going where?" the cop asked.

"One goin' each way. Well, she—" he had started to raise his hand to indicate the woman on the table but his hand dropped back to his side. "—she ran out there an' the one comin' from N'York knock right into her goin' thirty or forty miles an hour."

"What's the name of this place here?" the cop demanded.

"Hasn't got any name."

Just then a well-dressed Negro stepped up. "It was a yellow car. Big yellow car. New."

And the picture started to focus for me. I turned from Nick to Tom and back to the Negro man.

"See the accident?" the cop asked.

"No, but the car passed me down the road, going faster'n forty. Going fifty, sixty."

A big yellow car.

"Come here and let's have your name. Look out now. I want to get his name."

A big yellow car. The circus car. I couldn't move and let my eyes travel back to that dead woman and then there was a sudden change in the scene—something stopped. And then I realized that the green man in the office swaying back and forth had stopped wailing "Oh My Ga-od!" Now he shouted, "You don't have to tell me what kind of car it was! I know what kind of car it was!"

Of course, he did. He filled it up with gas. But Tom reacted quickly, striding over to the office, his entire body stiff with muscles, and grabbed the man firmly by the upper arms.

"You've got to pull yourself together."

Pull yourself together. The man collapsed before Tom, but Tom held him up.

"Listen," Tom whispered firmly, almost shaking him. "I just got here a minute ago, from New York. I was bringing you that coupé we've been talking about. That yellow car I was driving this afternoon wasn't mine, do you hear? I haven't seen it all afternoon."

Covering himself. Covering all of us. That's what we always do, our set, cover ourselves. The only ones who could really hear Tom were Nick and me and the Negro man, who still stood there wide-eyed watching everything.

"What's all that?" the cop suddenly asked, eyeing Tom and that man.

"I'm a friend of his," Tom explained, keeping his hands on him, but turning toward the cop. "He says he knows the car that did it.... It was a yellow car."

The cop looked suspiciously at Tom. "And what color's your car?"

"It's a blue car, a coupé."

"We've come straight from New York," Nick added.

"That's right," a nondescript man said behind us. "I was behind them. The three of them."

The cop turned away at that. "Now if you'll let me have that name again correct—"

Tom literally picked up the green man—what was his name? ... Wilson—and carried him back into the office and set him down in a chair like some misbehaving child.

"If somebody'll come here and sit with him!" Tom called out.

Two other men who had been standing nearby look at each other and sauntered in the office. Tom shut the door behind him and without glancing at the body on the table walked past us. "Let's get out."

I stared once again at the body while Tom elbowed his way through the crowd back into the night air. A doctor, hurrying with a black bag in hand, pushed through the crowd from the opposite direction. All hopeless. Everything that moment seemed beyond hope.

Nick, too, stared at the body with an inexplicable expression clouding his face. Then it struck me. Tom standing at the table looking down at the body. Tom grabbing Wilson to calm him down. That dead woman was Tom's girl in town.

We climbed back into the blue coupé. Tom drove slowly away from the scene until he got around the bend and then slammed his foot down hard on the accelerator. I gaped straight ahead at the onrushing darkness. I felt his arm tremble and heard a sob and saw that Tom was crying. So it's all true. All true.

"The God Damn coward!" Tom cried. "He didn't even stop his car."

I couldn't think. I didn't want to think. And then we were back at the house. Tom stopped the car at the porch and looked up at two windows on the second floor, two square blocks of light tangled up with the ivy.

"Daisy's home," he murmured.

As we climbed out of the car, Tom looked at Nick and frowned slightly. "I ought to have dropped you in West Egg, Nick. There's nothing we can do tonight."

Is there anything more to do than step through the wreckage of this entire day?

As we stepped up the porch, he said, "I'll telephone for a taxi to take you home, and while you're waiting you and Jordan better go in the kitchen and have them get you some supper—if you want any." He opened the front door. "Come in."

Nick hesitated and studied the open door. "No thanks. But I'd be glad if you'd order me that taxi. I'll wait outside."

I put my hand on his arm. "Won't you come in, Nick?"

"No thanks."

He looked withdrawn. He would go home to his cottage. And where will I go? To my room. You would think he would want to speak to me, speak to me now about what he was thinking and what he knew and what he thought we should do.

"It's only half past nine," I said.

His withdrawn look hardened into an isolated look. He blinked at me and in the blink, I knew he had included me in this entire mess when I had done nothing at all—nothing beyond a slight push toward what would have happened anyway. Nick had abandoned me. Well, then, the hell with Nick. The hell with all of them. I removed my hand from his arm, turned, and trotted up the steps and into the house.

I stood in the high hallway, clutching my cape, and just stood there as Tom closed the door and mechanically called to the butler to ring up a taxi for Nick. I pulled the hat off my head and stood there clutching that as well.

Coming up beside me, Tom said, "It's been a hell of a day, hasn't it?"

His voice was surprisingly soft, gentle. Facts and events and the entire situation had flown out of his control or any possible control anyone could have had. There was no violence or aggression left in Tom that night.

"It's been a hell of a summer, I would say," I said to him.

He nodded. "Have some supper, Jordan. I'm going upstairs to talk to Daisy. We'll be down in a moment."

He left me standing there as he climbed the stairs to the second floor. I didn't want to eat anything, even though I felt empty and hungry. Nick's refusal to come in for something to eat had upset me more than I realized. Done with the day. Done with me. Done with us all.

I wandered down to the parlor, where I first met Mr. Nick Carraway and when this summer seemed to have begun—that single June night a couple of months ago but which now seemed endlessly far away.

I gazed at the enormous white couch in the darkness. The longest day of the year. Do you always look for the longest day of the year and then miss it? Well, Daisy, you didn't miss it. You just lived it. You just *had* the longest day of the year or of the decade or of the century.

I heard Tom and Daisy coming down the stairs, whispering to each other. Still standing in the doorway, I turned to them when they reached the bottom of the stairs.

"Will you have some supper with us, Jordan?" Daisy asked, her eyes pale.

I shook my head. "I think it's time this good girl got to bed."

Daisy's eyes melted into resignation. She knew that I, too, have had enough of this day and of her and of Tom and of Gatsby. I have had enough.

"Are you sure, Jordan?" Tom asked quietly.

"I'm quite sure."

Tom nodded.

Before they turned away, I said, "Daisy?"

"Yes, Jordan?"

"You didn't miss the longest day of the year."

She gazed at me in silence, and then she just turned away.

Chapter VII

At noon I called Nick.

Last night, after Daisy and Tom had gone into the kitchen for supper, I climbed the stairs and walked down the hall to my room, dropped my hat and cape on the floor, pulled off my white dress and threw it on a chair. I didn't turn on a single lamp in my room. I preferred the silky darkness, the sultry evening.

I stepped over to the open window and looked out at the night and listened to the dark sounds the night makes ... when I saw Nick walking back toward the house. Was he coming to talk to me? To make sure I was okay? A fragile hopefulness stood up within me, but he walked past the front door and the porch to the side of the house where the kitchen and pantry and side entrance were, and I couldn't see him anymore. I waited for a while but heard nothing. He must have gone to speak to Tom ... about something. He did not come to speak to me. My face tightened as sorrow and anger and frustration struck me, swiftly, quickly, as Gatsby's car must have struck that poor woman. I cried. I sobbed.

I fell into my four-poster bed and tried to sleep as images from the day, images from the summer throbbed in my head. I suppose I slept, but I can't recall and then it was morning. Wondrous light lifted the room into color.

I gathered up my belongings, went downstairs, and called a taxi from the hall telephone. After I made the call, I saw Daisy standing at the top of the stairs—she heard me on the telephone. Her face was haggard and pale as she looked down at me and my suitcases with a look of resigned understanding. She knew that I had to get out of there and away from them and their loves and their troubles.

"Tom and I are going away for a while," she said.

She seemed so small and so fragile. I went up to her. We both sat down on the step.

"Oh, Jordan," she sighed and told me everything.

I said nothing in response, and then she disappeared into the vast rooms of the mansion.

The taxi drove me over to Hempstead.

I called Nick. When I heard his voice on the phone, I said hello. His response was slow and sleepy, wary.

"I've left Daisy's house," I said as brightly as I could. "I'm at Hempstead and I'm going down to South Hampton this afternoon."

"Are you." His voice was formal.

"You weren't so nice to me last night."

"How could it have mattered then?"

I did not respond for a moment. It could have mattered a great deal to me. "However—I want to see you." I did need to talk.

"I want to see you too," Nick said, but his voice was closed-in on itself, as closed-in as his expression had been last night.

"Suppose I don't go to South Hampton and come into town this afternoon?"

"No—I don't think this afternoon."

No? What was he going to do? "Very well."

"It's impossible this afternoon. Various—"

And Nick talked about business briefly but never addressing the fact that I needed really to talk to him, to sort things out, and then we just weren't talking anymore. The phones were hung up.

I sat in a chair and stared at the telephone. And I thought about telephones and how Daisy had first talked to Nick Carraway that morning and invited him over for dinner, how the telephone rang during dinner when Tom's girl called, how I had called Nick all those times to let him know where I was since I moved around from house to house and place to place. And now it was over. The conversation died between us. Died from the moment he answered the phone. And what we had—whatever it was—had also died.

I felt empty and sad and angry and dizzy all at the same time. For a brief moment, Daisy's desire to be a beautiful little fool made much sense. I had been a fool. I had made a mistake about Nick and his Boy Scout honor and his moral imperialism. Nick was a bad driver too. He was as bad a driver as I was. In fact, all of us—Daisy, Tom, Gatsby—were all bad drivers.

Still ... I wondered if I would ever talk to Nick Carraway again.

I had been a fool.

We, all of us, had been fools.

Fools.

Biographical Note

Ted Wojtasik is the author of two novels, *No Strange Fire* and *Collage*, and many short stories published in various literary journals, most recently in *Cold Mountain Review*. His first novel received a Silver Angel Award from Excellence in Media and a gold-starred review and "Editors' Choice" in *Booklist* in 1996. His second novel was one of five finalists for the Lambda Literary Award in 2004. He served on the Literature Panel for the National Endowment of the Arts in 2003. His short story "Scars and Frost" received honorable mention in *O. Henry Festival Stories 2000*, a short story competition, sponsored by Greensboro College in North Carolina. He is also a playwright having had three of his one-act plays produced at the Gilbert Theater in Fayetteville: "Cold but Soft," "A 1965 Thunderbird," and "Tender Moments." He is a visiting faculty member of English and Creative Writing at St. Andrews University in Laurinburg, North Carolina. He holds a B.A. in philosophy from George Washington University, an M.F.A. in fiction writing from Columbia University and a Ph.D. in English from the University of South Carolina.

Made in the USA
Las Vegas, NV
04 April 2021

20820427R00085